DISNEP
BEDTIME
STORIES

Adapted by Helena Mayer

Based on the Screenplay by Matt Lopez and Tim Herlihy

And the Story by Matt Lopez

Executive Producers Adam Shankman, Jennifer Gibgot, Garrett Grant,
Ann Marie Sanderlin

Produced by Adam Sandler, Jack Giarraputo, Andrew Gunn

Directed by Adam Shankman

DISNEP PRESS

New York

Prologue

I'm going to tell you a story now.

But as any good storyteller knows—and I am a *very* good storyteller—there are several vitally important things that must be done before one begins. First off, one must be sure the audience (that's you) is ready. Are you comfortably seated? Do you need to use the bathroom? What's that? You do?

Too bad. Hold it in.

So now we will begin as we begin every

story—with a certain phrase. A magical phrase filled with awesome and mysterious power. Ready?

Here we go.

Once upon a time . . .

Chapter One

Once upon a time, there was a man named Martin Bronson. He was the owner and operator of the Sunny Vista Motel, which he established on the corner of Sunset and La Cienega boulevards in Los Angeles, California, USA. This was in the year 1974. It was a labor of love for Marty, and he ran the hotel with the help of his children, Wendy and Skeeter.

Wendy wasn't a huge fan of the hospitality

business, but for Skeeter the motel was a magical place. He could bounce on the beds in the empty rooms. He could wage fierce battles with his armies of minisoaps and shampoos. He could explore wild, exotic new territories . . . like the ice room. Or the snack bar.

Wherever he went, he was surrounded by happy guests. Glowing honeymooners, cheerful businessmen, laughing families—all of them pleased to be spending a night at the Sunny Vista Motel.

There was only one problem. Marty Bronson was a wonderful dad, a splendid host . . . but a terrible businessman. His old-fashioned ideas about hospitality didn't stand a chance in such a cutthroat field. Before long, the Sunny Vista was on its last legs. Marty did everything he could to save the business.

And even though he was only eight years old, little Skeeter tried his best to help. "I've got a lot of ideas about how to improve things around here," he said one night as his dad was tucking him into bed. "I was thinking we could put an extra pair of socks in each room, 'cause people always forget to pack enough socks when they go on a trip."

Marty smiled warmly as he pulled the covers up to Skeeter's chin.

"Wait, Dad, I'm not even tired!" Skeeter protested. "Maybe if you tell me one of your bedtime stories, it'll make me fall asleep."

Marty thought about it for a moment, then sat down on the edge of the bed. He could tell a pretty fair tale when the muse was with him. He assumed a suitably dramatic storytelling voice, and within moments, little Skeeter was swept away to magical, imaginary lands. By the time Marty finished the story, Skeeter was asleep.

Or so Marty thought.

As soon as Marty left, Skeeter's eyes popped open. He climbed from his bed and slipped out of his room, tiptoeing down the hallway toward his father's office. He stopped just outside the door, peering inside.

His father was in there, talking to a British man that Skeeter had never seen before. Skeeter had no way of knowing that this was Barry Nottingham, one of the world's most successful young hotel owners. "Can't you read the writing on the wall, Bronson?" Mr. Nottingham asked. "This motel is sinking in red ink, and I'm offering you a last lifeboat."

Mr. Nottingham handed Marty Bronson a piece of paper and a pen. Marty gripped the pen and held it over the page, then he froze.

"Oh, for goodness sake!" Mr. Nottingham snapped. "I've never met a more indecisive man in my life. You've got to have confidence to succeed in this business! And you have none!"

Yet Marty was still hesitant. He said he had hoped to pass the Sunny Vista on to Skeeter one day.

"I understand, Bronson," Mr. Nottingham said, slinging an arm around Marty's shoulder. "How about this—if your boy works hard and shows some smarts when he grows up, I'll let him run the place for me someday." Mr. Nottingham dropped his arm—and, at the same time, dropped the friendly act. "Now sign the darn papers!"

Heaving a long sigh, Marty signed his name at the bottom of the contract—and lost the Sunny Vista Motel forever.

"That's my boy, Bronson," Mr. Nottingham said heartily. "Trust me, I'm going to turn this place into the best hotel in Los Angeles. It's gonna be uptight and outta-sight!"

And he kept that promise. . . .

Like an ugly duckling becoming a beautiful swan, the Sunny Vista motel metamorphosed into a huge, luxurious, and—yes—uptight and outta-sight new hotel: the Sunny Vista Nottingham. For thirty years, it reigned supreme as the place where princes and presidents stayed when visiting Southern California. And if those princes and presidents needed anything, they asked for Skeeter Bronson . . . the handyman.

You thought I was going to say 'manager,' didn't you?

So did Skeeter. Or, at least, he kept waiting for

Barry Nottingham to say "manager," giving him the promotion he dreamed of.

He'd been waiting for a long time.

Skeeter had been working at the hotel his entire life. He started out as a parking valet, then room-service waiter, then apprentice handyman, then got bumped up to assistant handyman. He'd been the chief handyman for three years. But that wasn't enough for Skeeter. He wanted to run the place, just like his father had all those years ago. And he was sure he'd be great at it. After all, the guests loved him.

For example, take the day he saw one of the receptionists yelling at an older woman. Skeeter couldn't just stand by and watch.

"Hi, Mrs. Dixon," Skeeter said, smiling warmly at the woman. "Is there something I can help you with?"

"Skeeter, this has nothing to do with you," the receptionist said. Her name was Aspen, and she hated Skeeter. (In fact, she pretty much hated everyone—except for her boss, Kendall Duncan.)

"Mrs. Dixon here has been taking bottles out of her minibar," Aspen sneered, "and now she doesn't want to pay for them."

Mrs. Dixon widened her eyes. "I didn't even open that evil little refrigerator!" she cried in a high, quivering voice.

Skeeter frowned. "Is it possible there was a mix-up?" he asked Aspen. "Maybe the minibar wasn't restocked with juice after the last guest checked out?"

Before Aspen could answer, the old woman shook her head so hard Skeeter was afraid her false teeth might pop out. "I saw who took it! He thought I was asleep, but I tricked him! He had red hair and a beard, and was wearing a green suit with brass buttons and a green bowler hat. He stood about ten inches tall."

Skeeter bit the corners of his lips, trying not to smile. "That sounds like a leprechaun," he said politely and turned back to Aspen. "My fault. My leprechaun traps must not be doing the trick. I'll pay for the missing juice myself." He turned back to Mrs. Dixon. "If you spot any more leprechauns, just dial eight eight. That's my direct line."

Aspen was *not* amused. She walked off in disgust.

"You've always taken such good care of your guests, Skeeter," Mrs. Dixon said. "Just like your father taught you."

"I try." Skeeter smiled fondly at the thought of the old days. "I'll tell you, my dad would have loved what they've done to this place."

Mrs. Dixon smiled. "Well, he provided the most important ingredient."

Skeeter looked confused. "What's that?"

Mrs. Dixon leaned close, a mysterious smile playing on her lips. "Why, magic, of course."

Chapter Two

You've probably been to a few birthday parties in your life. And I'm guessing these parties had some things in common. Kids. Birthday cake. Fun. In fact, you probably thought a birthday party was *required* to have those things.

Think again.

Bobbi Duva's birthday party had plenty of kids. It had a cake . . . sort of. But as far as Bobbi was concerned, it was missing one big thing: fun.

Not that her mother, Wendy Bronson-Duva, had caught on. "Um, I notice nobody's eating the gluten-free wheatgrass cake!" she cried. "Trust me, it is delicious!"

"We like it, Mom," said a cheerful voice. That was Patrick, Wendy's son. He was at the table with his sister and was gulping down mouthfuls of cake.

"I know you do, my sweeties," Wendy said. "Bobbi, why don't you go play with your friends?"

Bobbi just shrugged and stared down at her plate. She didn't have many real friends—and it wasn't just because her mom always served gluten-free wheatgrass cake. Bobbi was the kind of kid no one really noticed. She had a lot to say—but she didn't like to say it out loud. It was easier for her to fade into the background.

Not like Patrick. Patrick liked to grin, he liked to tell jokes, he liked to swing upside down on the jungle gym—he even liked gluten-free wheatgrass cake.

You may be wondering why it matters that Bobbi Duva didn't have many friends or that Patrick Duva was on his fourth slice of cake. Someone who *didn't* know that I was a world-class storyteller might worry that I'd fallen asleep at the wheel and accidentally dumped you into the wrong story.

Be assured that I'm *very* good at my job. Right now my job is to tell you that there's a reason I'm telling you all this.

And that reason just walked in the door.

Skeeter didn't ring the bell. He just pushed his way into the house, carrying a plastic bag in one hand and a present in the other.

"Please tell me you've got some kind of food in that bag," one of the kids from the party said, rushing up to him.

Skeeter shrugged. "Just some chocolate-chip cookies—"

The kid snatched the bag out of his hands and waved it in the air. "Fooooooooood!" he called to the other party guests.

The room erupted into screams. The kid with the cookies ran out, and the rest of the party chased after him. By the time Wendy Bronson-Duva showed up, she and Skeeter were alone.

Skeeter grinned at his sister. The grin made him look just like his nephew Patrick. Wendy didn't grin back.

"You've got to bring sugary, chemical-filled crud to my house every time you visit?"

"Every time I visit? I haven't been here in four years," Skeeter protested.

"It has *not* been four years, Skeeter! Remember, you were here for the Fourth of July barbecue? When you punched my husband?"

"Yeah, that was four years ago." Skeeter looked a little embarrassed. "But he was asking for it. And he's your *ex*-husband."

Wendy flinched. "Thanks for bringing *that* up."

Skeeter felt bad for reminding her. He wanted to say something to make his sister feel better. But he was pretty sure whatever he said would be wrong. It was always like that with him and Wendy. That's why he hadn't seen her kids in four years. He couldn't believe how much they had changed.

"Hey, kids!" he said. "Remember me? Uncle Skeeter?"

Patrick stared blankly at him. Bobbi didn't even look up from her cake.

"You guys were pretty young last time I saw you." He handed the gift to Patrick. "Happy birthday, Bobby."

"That's Bobbi," Patrick said, jerking a thumb at his sister.

"Whoa, my bad," Skeeter said, deciding he was officially the worst uncle in the history of uncles. "So, how's school? It must be pretty weird when your mom is the principal. Your teachers are probably terrified of you." Skeeter put on a stuttery, scared, teacher voice. "No h-h-h-h-homework for you, Bobbi! Take extra r-r-r-recess, Patrick! I don't want no problem with your mama."

They smiled. Just a little, but it was a start.

"Skeeter!" Wendy waved him over. "Please don't talk about school with them," she said.

"Why? What's with the school?" Skeeter asked.

"They're closing it down. I'm getting laid off."

"No way!" Skeeter replied. "But you're the classic school principal. You're tough and scary and bad with people."

Wendy glared at him. Her lower lip trembled. Uh-oh.

"I'm sorry. That came out wrong," Skeeter quickly added. "What else can you do? I guess you could be a dictator."

Wendy sighed. "I've got some interviews set up in Arizona. Actually, I kind of wanted to talk to you about that. I need you to watch the kids . . . for a week."

Skeeter swallowed hard. A whole *week*? "I was wondering why you invited me over."

"It won't be that difficult," Wendy explained,

sounding desperate. "My friend Jill is a teacher at my school, so she can bring the kids in with her in the morning, then watch them until dinnertime. You'll just have the night shift."

"These guys don't want to be with me. They don't even like me. Besides, why can't your goofy friend put them to bed?" Skeeter didn't have to meet Jill to know she'd be goofy. *All* Wendy's friends were goofy.

"She's got night school." Wendy's lip trembled again. "Skeeter, my husband left me, I'm getting laid off, I have to move—I need help. And you know it's not easy for me to ask anyone for help."

"Especially your little brother." It was funny how talking to Wendy could make Skeeter feel like he was ten years old all over again.

"Especially my little brother," Wendy agreed.

Even though they didn't always get along, Wendy was still his sister. Bobbi and Patrick were still his niece and nephew. Skeeter wanted to help. "Yeah, of course I'll do it. We are gonna have fun!" he promised the kids. "Wahoo! Maybe we can go fishing or something."

"I'd rather you didn't," Wendy said primly. "Patrick's not a strong enough swimmer."

"Fine. We'll stay inside. I'll teach you guys how to play poker."

Wendy's eyes almost bugged out of her head. "*Gambling?* Are you kidding me?"

Skeeter gritted his teeth. "Maybe we can take some walks in the park and catalog plant species."

Wendy nodded. "Now we're talking."

Skeeter shrugged and shook his head. "I don't know anything about plant species except the plastic ones last longer."

The kids burst into laughter.

Yes! Skeeter thought. They like me. "I better get out of here before your birthday guests smell the Cinnabons I got in the car." He figured it was best to quit while he was ahead. "Good luck on your trip, sis, and I'll see you punks . . . ?" He looked at Wendy to finish the sentence for him.

"Monday night," Wendy added.

"Monday night!" He gave his sister a kiss on the cheek. He didn't know how to say good-bye to the kids. A handshake was too formal, but he didn't feel right hugging them—they barely knew who he was. So he just patted their heads and mumbled a good-bye.

Outside, there was a woman pacing in front of his car. Well, maybe *car* was the wrong word for it. Other people drove cars. Skeeter drove a pickup truck. A giant, bright green monster of a truck that would have looked ready for a monster truck rally . . . if it weren't covered with Sunny Vista Nottingham logos.

"This your truck, chief?" the woman asked. Her cheeks glowed red with anger.

"Yes, ma'am," said Skeeter. Something about her announced: *I'm in charge.*

"Do you realize it's taking up two parking spaces?" she asked.

"It's a big truck, ma'am," Skeeter said politely.

"It's not that big, sir," the woman said. Her

voice was polite, too—but only on the surface. "You could fit into one spot."

Skeeter gave her a nervous grin. "Well, here's the thing: it's not really mine. It belongs to the hotel I work for. So I can't get a scratch on it. And two parking spaces provides what I call a 'cushion of protection.'"

"A hotel?" The woman took a closer look at him. She clearly didn't like what she saw. "You must be Wendy's brother. I'm Jill."

Jill? Skeeter's face was expressionless. Did he know anyone named Jill?

"Her friend?" Jill prompted him. "The one who's helping you watch the kids next week? I'm on the day shift."

"Oh. Okay," Skeeter said, remembering the goofy friend Wendy had told him about. He supposed he should try to chat with her. "Do you plan to be this hostile the whole time?"

Jill looked like she was deciding whether to laugh or to bonk him on the head. "Depends on if you keep that haircut."

Skeeter unlocked his truck door. "Didn't you hear? Goofy is the new handsome."

He could already tell this babysitting thing was going to be an even bigger hassle than he'd thought.

Chapter Three

Skeeter didn't get to spend a lot of time in the luxurious Sunny Vista Nottingham ballroom . . . unless he was fixing stuff.

"Time is of the essence here, Skeeter," Kendall Duncan snapped, as Skeeter did some emergency electrical surgery on a microphone cable behind the central podium. Kendall Duncan was the hotel's manager, and he was uptight on a normal day. This was no normal day. The ballroom was packed, and Barry Nottingham was due to make a major speech—*if* Skeeter could get the microphone working in time.

"Just want to make sure the big boss doesn't get himself electrocuted," Skeeter said, wrapping duct tape around the wire. He grabbed the mic. "Testing, one-two, one-two." His voice echoed throughout the ballroom. "Checkety-check-check-check. I say Barry, you say Nottingham," he chanted. "Barry!"

"Nottingham!" the audience shouted back.

"Barry!" Skeeter yelled.

"Nottingham!" the audience cheered.

Skeeter handed the microphone over to the hotel owner. "Got 'em riled up for you, sir," Skeeter said. "You're good to go."

"Uh, fantastic," Mr. Nottingham said. "Thank you, Sandy."

"It's Skeeter." He held out his hand. "It's good to see you again, Mr. Nottingham."

The hotel owner frowned and jerked away from Skeeter's outstretched hand. "Germs!" he yelped.

Kendall sucked in a horrified breath and then hustled Skeeter away from the podium. "Mr. Nottingham has developed a fear—not a fear, an awareness—of germs," he explained quietly, "and how dangerous they can be when not . . . properly, uh . . . feared."

"Oh." Skeeter glanced at the big boss. "That explains the plastic pants."

Mr. Nottingham stepped up to the podium and looked out at the ballroom full of familiar faces. "I bring you exciting news," he announced. "As you know, I own twenty-three hotels, from Berlin to Beijing, but it's no secret that this one, the Sunny Vista Nottingham, is my favorite. We've been sprucing up this grand old lady for years, but there are some who feel this is a losing battle—myself included. And so we have decided to close this hotel and build . . ." He walked over to a large object hidden beneath a sheet. ". . . the Sunny Vista *Mega*Nottingham."

He whipped off the sheet, revealing a detailed, 3-D model of a huge hotel. "It will be the largest hotel on the West Coast," Mr. Nottingham said proudly, showing off all the different features. "Eighteen-hundred rooms, five restaurants, six European-style discotheques, three swimming pools, three theaters, and a top secret theme that will blow your minds."

The room exploded into applause. Even Skeeter was blown away.

So blown away, in fact, that he didn't notice the beautiful British woman standing next to him. (And it wasn't normal for Skeeter not to notice a beautiful woman.)

"I simply don't understand all this fuss," the woman said softly. "It's just a big building."

"No, this is the future of the hotel business," Skeeter said exuberantly. "My dad said one day the Sunny Vista could be the biggest hotel in Los Angeles. And now it's actually happening!"

"A project of this size simply will not fit on our current site," Mr. Nottingham continued. "But we have gone to contract on a breathtaking parcel nearby and plan on breaking ground before the end of the month." He paused for another round of applause. "I'm sad to announce that Ron Strickler, our longtime general manager here, will not be making the move with us. His departure creates an opportunity for the younger generation to step forward and assume the role of leadership. And so I'm proud to announce the new hotel's general manager. We all know him, we know how hard he works, how intelligent he is, how much this hotel means to him . . ."

An electric shock ran through Skeeter's body. Was this what it felt like when your dream came true? Was Mr. Nottingham about to say his name?

"The man behind all these great new ideas . . ." Mr. Nottingham continued, *"Kendall Duncan."*

"Kendall?" Skeeter muttered under his breath. He couldn't believe it. "How can that English muffin pick a phony like Kendall to run this hotel?"

"English muffin," the British woman next to him repeated. She giggled. "Funny, I've never heard anyone call my father that."

Skeeter's eyes widened. Did she say *father*?

A moment later, Mr. Nottingham himself appeared by the woman's side. "So, what do you think, Violet?"

Violet Nottingham quickly shot Skeeter a mischievous look. "Why . . . it's the future of the hotel business, Daddy."

Mr. Nottingham beamed.

"Oh, hello there," he said, finally noticing Skeeter. "Do you know my daughter, Violet?"

"Only by reputation, sir." In a flash, Skeeter ran through all the things he knew about Violet Nottingham—and thanks to the tabloids, he knew quite a lot. "I mean, not that she has a 'reputation' . . . I heard she was hot . . . uh, not hot. *Beautiful.* And she likes to go out and have festive, fun times. In bars."

Skeeter Bronson was pretty good at the handyman thing, but when it came to saying the wrong thing, he was a world champion.

"That's the *old* Violet Nottingham," Kendall said, joining the others and stepping between

Skeeter and Violet. He wrapped his arms around her. "Before she met *me*. I'm going to keep my pookie bear out of the clubs and out of the tabloids."

Violet and Kendall, *together*? Skeeter couldn't believe it. What would a beautiful, funny, amazing woman like Violet be doing with a man like . . . *Kendall*?

Violet smiled at Skeeter. Her smile was like the sun—and he felt like ice cream, melting into a puddle of goo at her feet. "Daddy thinks being here in the States with my honey will keep me on the straight and narrow." She glanced down at her cell phone, and her perfect lips formed a perfect O-shape of horror. "Uh-oh, I'm late! Nice meeting you, Skeeter."

Skeeter wanted to say that it had been *more* than nice to meet her. It had been wonderful. Spectacular. Mind-blowing. But by the time he'd decided on the exact right word, she was gone.

Chapter Four

The Sunny Vista Nottingham had more than two hundred rooms. Each of them had a soft mattress, fluffy pillows, gilded paintings on the walls, lush carpeting, bright curtains, and a huge, luxurious bathtub. Each surface gleamed; each sheet and pillow smelled like a fresh summer morning. You could say that each room in the Sunny Vista Nottingham was a work of art. Each of them, that is, except Skeeter's.

Skeeter sat in his room in a messy cabana. He

was slouched in a wobbly, rusted chair, gulping down fries.

He'd spent his day staring at the peeling paint on the wall, wondering if he would be a hotel handyman for the rest of his life. If only he could come up with some way of proving himself to Barry Nottingham.

But by the time his friend Mickey, a room-service waiter, had shown up with dinner, Skeeter still hadn't come up with a single idea.

"So did you demand that he make you the big boss of the new hotel?" Mickey asked, sitting down and helping himself to some fries. "He promised your pop! Why didn't you hold him to it?"

Skeeter pushed the fries back and forth on his plate. "I don't know. It didn't seem like the right time."

"You know why the big man's giving the job to Kendall: he's dating his daughter. That's how it works in the business world—keep it in the family. He gets the job, the girl, the everything."

Skeeter felt like bashing his head against the table. "Thanks for cheering me up."

The phone rang before Mickey could respond. (Which was probably a good thing—when it came to cheering people up, Mickey wasn't what you'd call an expert.)

"You're still *there*?" a woman's voice said when Skeeter picked up. She sounded mad, whoever she was.

"I answered the phone, didn't I?" Skeeter was not in the mood for some kind of prank call. "Who is this?"

"Look, I've got to get to class," the woman said. "The kids are waiting for you."

That's when it hit him. It was Monday night. He was supposed to pick Wendy's kids up from that woman.

This woman on the phone.

And he was already an hour late.

"Be there in twenty." Skeeter snapped the phone shut. "One night off, and I gotta go babysit my niece and nephew," he explained to Mickey as he hunted around the cabana for his coat. "Any advice?"

Mickey shoved a few more fries into his mouth. "Sometimes, I babysit my cousins. They like it when I let them style my hair—you know, make braids, put beads in there, stuff like that."

Skeeter's face was blank for a second.

"Hey," he said at last. "Can I have some of those fries?"

Mickey handed over a few french fries.

"And some ketchup?" He reached over and rubbed the fries in a blob of ketchup. Then he gave Mickey the only response he could think of to his babysitting advice—he threw the drippy fries in his face.

Mickey just laughed. "Your plan backfired!" he called to Skeeter, who was on his way out the door. "I love ketchup in the face!"

Chapter Five

Babysitting wasn't as tough as Skeeter had expected. Maybe because he sent the kids straight to bed as soon as he arrived.

"All right, so you guys cool?" Skeeter asked, as Bobbi and Patrick slipped under the covers.

Bobbi ignored him.

"You have to read us a bedtime story," Patrick said.

"I do? Oh . . . okay." How hard could that be?

Skeeter grabbed a pile of books from a nearby shelf and looked for a title that sounded cool. *"Rainbow Crocodile Saves the Wetlands? Web Design Basics for Kids? The Organic Squirrel Gets a Bike Helmet?"* What kind of bedtime stories were those? "Don't you have any *real* stories?"

Patrick looked confused. "Like what?"

Skeeter shrugged. "You know, cowboys and dragons and aliens and whatnot, like every other kid in the world goes to sleep to?"

Patrick and Bobbi were giving him a weird look. But Skeeter had a funny feeling the look had nothing to do with what he was saying. Actually, Skeeter had a funny feeling, period. "Can somebody tell me *what just crawled onto my head*?" he said slowly, trying not to freak out.

"That's Bugsy," Patrick said. "Our guinea pig."

There's a rodent on my head, Skeeter thought. Okay. No time to freak out. He took a deep breath and very, very slowly, raised his hands to his head. He clamped them around a warm, squirmy body with sharp claws.

Gotcha! He pulled Bugsy off his head and took a closer look. It was actually kind of . . . cute. Especially his big, bulging bug eyes.

"All right," Skeeter said, once the guinea pig was safe and sound in its cage. "Let me try to make up a story like my old man used to."

And with that, Skeeter began. . . .

Once upon a time, in a magical, faraway kingdom, there was a brave and noble knight. He was a man of the people—strikingly handsome, smart, and a really hard worker. Everyone thought he was the man.

Actually, they didn't.

No one thought he was the man. They should have, but they didn't.

No, this man was actually . . . a peasant. His name was Mr. Underappreciated.

"What's underdemeciated?" Patrick interrupted.

"Sorry, I forgot you were six," Skeeter said. "His name was . . . Sir Fixalot." He went on.

Sir Fixalot was known far and wide for his many good deeds. He would rescue people who couldn't sleep because there were trolls under their beds and help them when they had problems with nasty troll-looking innkeepers. And then there was the time he fought off five mad mud monsters at one time. He would do anything to make sure people always had unclogged bathtub drains—and he always listened sympathetically to complaints about the porridge being too hot.

But, alas, the kingdom where Sir Fixalot lived did not place much value on dedication and hard work. Because the superstar in all the land was Sir Buttkiss. He was good-looking, he went to a top-notch knight college, and he spent his days kissing everyone's butt.

Now, this land had a king, and the king lived in mortal terror of these mysterious creatures called germs. The king had a beautiful daughter, Princess Fashionista. She loved to let loose and party but was dissuaded from doing so by her boyfriend, Sir Buttkiss.

And Sir Fixalot had a best friend, Friar Fred, who was not right in the head.

"Were there any kids in the kingdom?" Patrick asked, breaking in once again.

"Oh. Yeah." Skeeter was getting so into his story that he'd almost forgotten his niece and nephew. "Of course!"

There were two young pages, Mistress Stinky and Master Smelly, and they helped Sir Fixalot with all his good deeds. And in return, he let them climb trees and eat junk food and have snowball fights when their uptight mother wasn't looking.

Patrick sat up in bed. "And don't forget— Jillian, Queen of the Fairies!"

"Queen of the Fairies?" Skeeter repeated in disgust. "I don't think so. If she's gotta be there, let's make her a giant, angry raven. And—"

"No, she should be a mermaid teacher!" Patrick insisted.

"Fine," Skeeter agreed. "A mermaid teacher." He continued with his story.

One day, the king invited all the knights to his castle. "I bring thee glad tidings," the king announced. "For on this day, I have chosen the knight who will serve as my closest advisor and bestest buddy. The man I have chosen is perhaps not one thou wouldst expect. My new champion is a humble sort who shuns the spotlight. . . ."

When he heard this, Sir Fixalot felt his heart clench. Was it possible? Was the king talking about . . . him?

". . . Who does good deeds without hope of glory," the king continued.

It can't be, Fixalot thought.

". . . Who works hard to make my kingdom glorious."

Fixalot was almost afraid to hope. But this was Sir Fixalot we're talking about—he wasn't afraid of anything. So hope he did.

The king beamed at the crowd. "My new champion is . . . Sir Buttkiss!"

A spotlight found Sir Buttkiss in the audience. The stuck-up knight bounded up to the stage. Confetti showered the crowd. The paparazzi swarmed, flashbulbs popped, and Sir Fixalot was nearly blinded by the reflection off Sir Buttkiss's shiny armor.

But he still saw Sir Buttkiss bow deeply to the king.

He saw Sir Buttkiss gently take the hand of the beautiful princess.

He saw Sir Buttkiss wave at the crowd and drink in their applause—applause that should have belonged to Sir Fixalot.

Poor Sir Fixalot had been passed over. He moved into a giant shoe, developed a bad case of athlete's face. Then he fell into a moat and was eaten by crocodiles.

Skeeter looked at the kids. "The end."

"The end?" Patrick gaped at his uncle. "That can't be the end!"

"Why not?" Skeeter asked.

Patrick crossed his arms and looked at Skeeter as if he should be able to figure it out for himself. "It's not happy."

"There's no happy endings in real life, dudes,"

Skeeter informed them. "The sooner you learn that, the better."

"It's not fair!" Bobbi shouted.

Skeeter flinched. Since when did Bobbi *shout*? Bobbi didn't even *talk*.

"I mean . . . shouldn't Sir Fixalot at least have a shot at being champion?" Bobbi asked shyly.

"A shot?"

"If Sir Fixalot's *better* than Sir Buttkiss," Bobbi said fiercely, "he should have a chance to prove it."

You bet he should, Skeeter thought. And so should I.

Skeeter didn't have any control over whether Mr. Nottingham gave him a chance. But he *did* have control over whether Sir Fixalot got a chance. What's the point of being the storyteller if you can't tell the story you want to hear?

"Yeah, forget all that stuff about living in a shoe and crocodiles," Skeeter said quickly. "What the king really said was . . ."

"*On second thought, there is another worthy*

knight in my kingdom, and it wouldn't be right unless he got a shot, too. Doesn't every man deserve a chance to prove his worth, especially a man as hardworking and dependable as . . . Sir Fixalot?"

Sir Fixalot bounded onto the stage—and the crowd went nuts!

Everyone celebrated in his own way. Friar Fred drop-kicked a booing goblin. Mermaid Jillian did one of those dolphin tail moves. And Stinky and Smelly did the Irish jig!

And then . . .

"It started raining gum balls," Patrick said, yawning. "The end."

"Raining gum balls?" That didn't sound like any story Skeeter had ever heard.

"Why not?" Patrick asked. "It's a bedtime story. Anything can happen."

Skeeter forced himself to smile. "In a story, maybe. But real life doesn't work like that. Believe me, I wish it did. I really wish it did."

Skeeter flipped off the light. He paused in the

doorway, listening to the kids' soft and even breathing as they dropped off to sleep. It was so easy when you were a kid, he thought. You believed in things like magic and happy endings. You believed that life really could be fair.

Then you grew up.

Chapter
Six

The next morning, Skeeter was summoned by Mr. Nottingham. The big boss was having a serious crisis: his TV was broken.

Skeeter took the elevator up to the very top floor, home of the presidential suite. It was the finest room in the hotel, complete with a Jacuzzi, a (broken) wall-sized flat-screen TV, and three grand pianos. Not that Skeeter got to see any of it. He stepped through the door—and into total darkness.

The lights were out, the shades were drawn, and Mr. Nottingham was nothing but a shadowy figure looming over the sofa. "Bronson," his voice echoed in the darkness, "the telly won't turn on."

"Let me take a tallyho at it." Skeeter didn't move. "Uh . . . where is it?"

"Over here," Mr. Nottingham said. Skeeter tried to follow his voice. "When indoors, I try to conduct my business in the dark whenever I can. Did you know germs reproduce eighty percent faster in bright light?"

"No, I—" Skeeter crashed into something hard and pointy. "Ow!"

Mr. Nottingham chuckled. "Watch out for that umbrella stand."

Too late.

Stretching his arms out in front of him, Skeeter did a zombie shuffle across the room. Finally, his hands closed around the edge of the television. He pulled out his tools, hoping he wouldn't accidentally drill his hand to the wall. "So . . . how's the new hotel coming?"

"Very well," Mr. Nottingham answered. "Still dealing with the city on building permits and whatnot. I wish I could tell you the *secret* theme, but it's so good we don't want anyone to steal it."

"I hear you, sir," Skeeter answered as he puttered with the TV.

"Okay. I'll tell you," Mr. Nottingham said as though Skeeter had been pressing him for the theme. "Brace yourself. It's . . . rock and roll! Vintage vinyl, music memorabilia in the lobby—"

"You mean like the Hard Rock?" Skeeter asked, confused. Why would Mr. Nottingham turn his biggest and best hotel into a copy of another chain?

"The what?" Mr. Notthingham asked.

"The Hard Rock Hotel. They use that rock and roll theme, too."

There was a long silence.

"Please tell me you're joking," said Mr. Nottingham, but he didn't sound like he was in the mood to laugh.

"Uh, no. They've been around for a while. It's

a chain." Skeeter didn't get it. Could Mr. Nottingham really be *that* clueless? "I think there's, like, ten of them."

"I am familiar with the Hard Rock hotels. I just thought they were . . . caveman-themed."

There was another pause, even longer this time. Skeeter held his breath, trying not to laugh.

Mr. Nottingham fumed. "Please get Kendall up here right away."

"Are you talking to me?" Skeeter asked, confused.

"No. I just used the intercom."

As they waited for Kendall to arrive, Skeeter kept himself entertained by waving a hand in front of his face, seeing if he could tell how many fingers he was holding up.

He couldn't.

"You wanted to see me, sir?" Kendall said, out of nowhere.

"Whoa, you scared me, man." Skeeter peered into the darkness. "How'd you get in here?"

"I turned off the lights in the hallways first

so Mr. Nottingham wouldn't be exposed to additional germ infestation." There was a crashing sound. "Ow."

"I'm very disappointed in you, Kendall," Mr. Nottingham said. He sounded angry. "This rock and roll idea of yours is old hat. We almost made a fatal mistake."

Maybe it was true that when you couldn't see, your other senses got stronger, Skeeter thought. Because he was pretty sure he could hear Kendall's heart thudding faster. And it definitely smelled like Kendall was starting to sweat.

"I . . . I was going to put our own spin on it," Kendall stammered. "But I'll get right to work on a new idea, sir."

"Yes, you will." Mr. Nottingham clapped his hands together sharply. "You know what, Skeeter? I'm starting to have a fuzzy recollection of making a promise to your father. And I think I'm going to give you a shot. If you can come up with a better theme than Kendall does, I'll let you run the new place."

Am I dreaming? Skeeter thought in disbelief. But despite the darkness, he was pretty sure he was awake.

"Uh . . . sir." Kendall sounded horrified. "I think I speak for Skeeter when I say that we are both fans of your rightfully famous sense of humor. But don't you think this is a rather cruel joke to play on a *maintenance worker*?"

"No, I don't," Mr. Nottingham said. "Mr. Bronson's been working for this company for twenty-five years. I'm beginning to realize that I may have underdemeciated him—"

"Underdemeciated?" Kendall asked.

"You know what I mean!" Mr. Nottingham said. "You can present your ideas to me at my birthday party this weekend. That'll be all, gentlemen. And watch out for my germ vaporizer on—"

CRASH.

Skeeter giggled. "You didn't watch out, Kendall, did you?"

He walked out of the suite feeling like he was

walking on air. No, *floating*. He floated down to the lobby, floated out to the parking lot, and then floated all the way to his car.

As he drove down the palm tree–lined streets, Skeeter turned up his radio and opened the sunroof. The sky was a clear, bright blue, traffic was moving, and he had a new shot at his dream—it felt like one of those days when *nothing* could go wrong.

As he stopped at a light, a blue sports car pulled up alongside him.

"Hey there, buddy," Skeeter called through the open window, giving the guy a friendly wave. "Beautiful car you got there."

"Thanks, champ," the guy called back. "If you wanna be the best, you gotta drive the best."

Skeeter nodded. It made sense. "I wanna be the best," he said. "What's a sweet ride like that cost, anyway?"

The guy in the sports car gave Skeeter's truck a quick look and shrugged. "Not as much as you think. I would say if you work the rest of your life, take the money you save, and times it by ten . . . you could afford the muffler." The guy burst into laughter and sped away.

"You don't know me!" Skeeter shouted after him, shaking his fist. "One day I'm gonna be king of this town!"

But the other car was long gone.

Good riddance, Skeeter thought. *Nothing* was going to ruin his perfect day. Not even a red light that refused to change color no matter how long he waited at the intersection.

BONK!

"Ow!" Skeeter rubbed the back of his head. Had a *rock* dropped through the sunroof? He glanced around the truck: there was a blue gum ball sitting on the passenger seat.

"Huh?" Skeeter looked up—just in time to see a tidal wave of gum balls falling from the sky. A million of them pelted him. It was a rainbow hailstorm! There were so many gum balls flooding into the truck that Skeeter couldn't get the sunroof shut. He tugged his coat over his head and jumped out, rummaging around in the back until he found his umbrella.

It wouldn't open!

He fought with the umbrella as gum balls pinged and ponged off his head. Once he finally got it open, he stood in the middle of the street, utterly confused. Now that he was safely under the umbrella, he could see where the storm was coming from. A concrete ribbon of highway wound overhead. A truck was stopped at the edge; its logo read SWEET TOOTH CANDY CO. A waterfall of gum balls tumbled through its open trailer door—and down to the street below.

Skeeter thought about the story he'd told with Bobbi and Patrick. Specifically, he thought about how it ended: *and then it started raining gum balls.*

No way, he told himself. Not possible.

Except here he was, standing under an umbrella on a perfectly sunny day, watching gum balls fall from the sky.

Chapter Seven

That night, when Jill dropped off the kids at Skeeter's bungalow, he couldn't think about anything but starting a new bedtime story.

"Hey there, chief," Jill said, handing him their overnight bag and Bugsy's cage. "Here's their stuff. Now, why do they have to sleep here?"

"'Cause I'm on call tonight, Jennifer," Skeeter said distractedly.

"It's Jill, Scooter," she corrected him. But

he had already closed the door in her face.

He crouched down, meeting his niece and nephew eye to eye. "Hey, guys, I gotta ask you something. Anything weird happen to you today?"

Patrick shrugged. "I had a substitute teacher with an eye patch."

"Okay." Skeeter hesitated. He didn't want to sound like a nutcase. "A *little* weird, but . . . did you guys have any, uh . . . gum-ball incidents?" He showed them a fistful of gum balls left over from that afternoon's "rain."

"We're not allowed to chew gum," Bobbi reminded him. Bobbi was a big believer in following the rules.

"Oh, yeah, right, of course," Skeeter said quickly. "So . . . wanna go to bed?"

Patrick scowled. "It's only five-thirty," he argued. "And we haven't had dinner."

So Skeeter did his job as a good uncle and a good babysitter and gave them dinner. Mickey joined them. (It was only fair, since he was the one who delivered the food.) On the menu: burgers, fries, and, of course, pizza.

Bobbi and Patrick had never eaten junk food before. And that wasn't the only thing they'd never tried.

"So you've never played video games?" Mickey asked.

Bobbi shook her head. "Mom says they rot your brain."

"And you've never had bacon?" Skeeter said.

Patrick wrinkled his nose. "What's bacon?"

Skeeter sputtered. No bacon? That was downright cruel!

"It's the fatty part of the hog, adjacent to the rear end," Mickey explained grossly. "But tasty, not like I just made it sound."

"And that's the first hamburger you've ever eaten in your lives?" Skeeter said quickly, before Mickey could turn them off bacon forever. "How was it?"

Bobbi glanced over his shoulder, like she expected to see her mother standing in the doorway before looking earnestly at Skeeter. "Life changing," she confessed.

Patrick still looked worried. "Mom's gonna kill us."

Skeeter tried not to laugh. "When she was your age, your mother ate loads of hamburgers in this very room!"

"She did?!" Patrick and Bobbi cried together.

"Looks like Crazy Eyes ate loads of burgers in the last ten minutes," Mickey said, pointing to the guinea pig, who was lying on his back on the table. Sure enough, he was more bug-eyed than ever, and now he was fat, too. While they were all looking at him, the rodent let out a loud burp.

Skeeter tried to shake off the grossness of the scene. "All right," he announced, "let's get you carnivores to bed. I've got a new story I want to try on you. You guys like cowboys and Indians?"

As Bobbi and Patrick climbed into bed, Skeeter began his tale. . . .

Jeremiah Skeets was a farmhand looking to

make a name for himself in the Old West. However, he was justifiably concerned that people would always think of him as "just a farmhand," because of his shabby appearance. He began to think his ratty old horse might not be helping matters any.

So Jeremiah moseyed over to the local horse-trading barn.

"Hello, sir," Jeremiah told the salesman. "I am interested in seeing your finest horse."

The salesman gave Jeremiah a serene smile. "My ancestors believed that the horse spirit came down from the mountain during the time of the fire wind. Many brave warriors walked the trail of the moon bear to—"

"Dude, I just want a horse," Jeremiah cut in.

The horse trader nodded. "I can do it." He clapped his hands together sharply. "Screaming Rooster!" he shouted to a coworker. "Bring out . . . Speeder."

Screaming Rooster appeared with the most awesome-looking red horse Jeremiah had ever seen. And, according to the sticker price, it cost *about a million times more than Jeremiah could ever hope to afford.*

"This is the finest horse I've ever laid eyes on, sir," Jeremiah said, gazing at the horse. "It would be hard not to respect a man riding such an exceptional animal. But I'm afraid it may be a bit out of my price range."

The horse trader grinned. His teeth glinted in the sun. "Tell you what, white bread, I'll make you a deal. I'll give you Speeder . . . for freeeeeee!"

The end.

Patrick sat up in bed. "A guy getting a free horse?" he complained. "That's not a good story."

"Yeah, it is," Skeeter argued. "It's a great story."

Bobbi wasn't buying it. "Why can't he do something a real gentleman would do? Like save a damsel in distress. Like this . . ." And Bobbi took over.

Jeremiah was riding Speeder when he heard the cry.

"Help! Someone!" It was a damsel, and she

sounded like she might be in distress! "Please!"

Yep. Definitely in distress.

Jeremiah galloped in the direction of her cries. He pushed the horse faster and faster, knowing he was the damsel's only hope. Soon, he came upon an overturned stagecoach and a wealthy, beautiful woman in fine petticoats. It was Miss Davenport, the daughter of the wealthiest man in all of the West—and she was being attacked by outlaws! As they advanced on her, she backed away, pressing herself against the wall of a cliff. It was a dead end—there was no escape.

"Okay, you wanna do that?" Skeeter cut in. "Fine. But can we make her English?" He thought of Violet Nottingham's lovely, honeyed voice. "I like the way they talk."

Bobbi shrugged. "Sure, I guess."

As Miss Davenport backed away from the outlaws, she stripped off her jewelry, piece by piece. Rings, bracelets, necklaces—one by one she tossed them out to the outlaws as they clamored for more.

"Over here, lady!" one shouted.

"Over here!" yelled another.

"To me!" a third shouted, stretching out his arms.

"Please, show mercy on a helpless woman alone in the Old West!" Miss Davenport begged them. But the outlaws refused to yield.

Jeremiah tugged on Speeder's reins, then pushed the horse forward, breaking through the circle of outlaws. They backed away from the magnificent steed.

"Care for a lift, ma'am?" Jeremiah asked.

Miss Davenport grabbed his hand. With one strong tug, he pulled her up onto his horse. Then he glared down at the outlaws. "Now, let's all give the pretty lady her stuff back."

One of the outlaws drew a gun—but Jeremiah, the fastest draw in the West, drew his faster. He shot the gun right out of the outlaw's hand.

The scoundrels dropped the jewels and ran away like the cowards they were.

Miss Davenport was impressed. "Why, thank you, fine gentleman."

Skeeter cleared his throat. He was ready to take over again. . . .

So Jeremiah spirited Miss Davenport away to safety. And Miss Davenport said, "How can I ever thank you, sir?"

"No thanks is necessary, ma'am." Jeremiah was a very humble guy. "The highest honor a gentleman can ever achieve is to rescue a beautiful damsel in distress."

"But I do insist on expressing my gratitude in some manner. I am a woman of considerable means, Jeremiah. Gold, jewels, real estate. Simply name it, and it is yours."

Jeremiah thought about it. For about ten seconds. "Fair enough. I'll take a hundred million dollars."

He may have been humble, but he wasn't stupid.

"The end," Skeeter said quickly, before Jeremiah could get into any more trouble. "Let's hope it works. Good night." He hopped off the bed, ready to slip out and wait for his new "horse" to arrive.

"Jeremiah wouldn't take money for doing a good deed!" Bobbi protested.

"Why not?" Skeeter shot back. Who would turn down free money?

Patrick sat up in bed. He looked very stern. It was the same expression Wendy got when Skeeter tried to slip the kids a sugar cookie. "Gentlemen don't get paid."

But *Skeeter* did. "Hey, who's telling the story here?"

Bobbi wouldn't let it drop. "It should really go more like this . . .

"That's mighty kind of you, Miss Davenport. But it would be unseemly to accept money as recompense for an act of virtue."

Miss Davenport bit her lip and thought very hard. "Well, I must give you some token of my appreciation. . . ."

Jeremiah shook his head and began to climb back on his horse.

"Perhaps . . . a kiss?" Miss Davenport said, looking up at Jeremiah.

He got off the horse.

She's beautiful, Jeremiah thought, gazing at Miss Davenport. So beautiful she almost glowed. She reached out for him. Their faces drew close. Jeremiah closed his eyes. He could almost feel her lips brush against his. And then, just as they were about to kiss . . .

"An angry dwarf kicks him in the butt!" Patrick shouted gleefully. "The end."

Bobbi burst into laughter and high-fived her brother.

Skeeter couldn't help grinning. "Okay, weirdos. I'll take a new ride and a kiss. I'll worry about the hundred million tomorrow night." He turned out their light. "Good night, kids. Sleep well." Babysitting wasn't so bad after all. He would almost be sorry when it was time for them to go home to their mother. And not just because, thanks to them, he was about to get a brand-new, top-of-the-line sports car.

Skeeter was starting to like these two.

Chapter Eight

Once the kids were asleep, Skeeter left Mickey in charge and ducked out for a quick trip to the nearest car dealership. The cars gleamed in the pale, reflected moonlight. He pressed his fingers to the glass, deciding on the fiery red car on the far left. It was a steed fit for a gentleman.

Skeeter suddenly noticed a burly guy lurking around the entrance of the dealership. Maybe this was it!

"Hey," Skeeter said, trying to contain his excitement.

The guy barely looked his way. "Hello."

Skeeter sidled closer. "Are you the man I'm supposed to see?" he whispered loudly.

The guy shrugged. "I'm here, aren't I?"

"Am I about to end up with that cherry red one right there?" Skeeter gently tapped the glass, pointing toward the red car in the showroom.

The guy shrugged again. "I don't see why not."

"For freeeeeeee?" Skeeter added.

"Sounds about right," the guy said.

I knew it! Skeeter thought. He forced himself to stay calm.

The guy didn't say anything else.

"So what happens now?" Skeeter finally asked. "Do I have to eat one of the gum balls or something?"

The guy tipped his head to the side, then nodded. "Yes."

It made as much sense as anything else.

Skeeter pulled a gum ball out of his pocket and popped it into his mouth. He bit down hard, once, twice, three times.

Nothing happened.

"Now what?" Skeeter asked.

"Close your eyes and count to six."

Skeeter closed his eyes. "One . . . two . . . three . . . four . . . five . . . six." He opened his eyes— just in time to see the guy running down the street with his wallet.

"Hey!" Skeeter took off after him. He got about three steps—before he tripped and fell flat on his face.

This was definitely not part of the plan.

Skeeter picked himself up and trudged back to his truck. I'll probably be riding around in this thing for the rest of my life, he thought gloomily, driving through the dark, empty streets.

He rounded a corner, and suddenly the street wasn't empty anymore. Flashbulbs popped as a horde of paparazzi chased after a shadowy figure. Skeeter peered through the windshield. There was something familiar about the figure. The flash-bulbs lit her up, and Skeeter gasped: it was Violet Nottingham!

"Boys, could you give me a break tonight?" Violet cried, hurrying away from the pack as fast as her stiletto heels could carry her. She raised her key chain in the air, frantically clicking the button that would unlock her car. A *beep-boop* rang out from somewhere in the distance. Violet turned on her heel, heading toward the sound.

The paparazzi chased after her.

"Over here!" they shouted. "Here, Violet!"

Violet ran faster, her heels clattering against the pavement. She veered left into an alley—but it was a dead end. She spun around: her only exit was blocked.

"Please!" she begged them. "Not tonight, okay? Can you just leave me alone one time?"

But it was no use. In the dark, their cameras flashing, their feet scraping against the pavement, they seemed barely human.

"To me!" the photographers shouted, each of

them trying to get Violet to turn in his direction. "Over here!"

"No! Over here, lady!"

"Hey, Violet!"

She pressed herself against the wall, pleading with them to stop. But it was no use—until Skeeter's truck thundered into the alley. All of the photographers scattered.

"Hey!" one of them shouted.

"What's your problem, man!" another cried.

"Jerk!"

Like a gentleman rescuing a fair lady, Skeeter swung open the passenger door and held out his arm to Violet. He knew exactly what to say. "Care for a lift, ma'am?"

Violet climbed into the truck. Skeeter glared down at the photographers. "Now let's give the pretty lady back all those pictures you just took."

"In your dreams, buddy," one of the angry photographers scoffed.

"You sure about that?" Skeeter grabbed something from the floor of his truck. In the dim light, it looked like a gun. He hit the gas pedal, and the truck backfired loudly.

BANG!

The terrified paparazzi threw their cameras on the ground and ran away. Violet gaped at Skeeter.

"Good thing they didn't make me use it," he said, showing her his "gun." It was just a drill.

"My hero," Violet said, laughing.

They drove down the dark street until Violet spotted her car. Skeeter stopped the truck and walked around to open the door for Violet. She smiled at him and carefully climbed out. "That was brilliant, Skeeter. Kendall could take some lessons from you. How can I ever thank you?"

Once again, Skeeter knew his lines. "No thanks is necessary, ma'am."

Violet batted her eyes. "Oh, am I in the presence of a gentleman?"

Was she flirting with him? No beautiful woman had ever done that before. "At your service, ma'am," Skeeter said, in a Jeremiah-like cowboy accent.

"Well, I must show my appreciation in some way. . . ." Violet gave him a secretive smile. She closed her eyes. Tilted her head. Pursed her lips.

Skeeter took a quick look over his shoulder: no angry dwarfs. Just a damsel, about to offer him the greatest reward known to any man alive, one perfect—

WHACK!

"Ow!" Skeeter yelped, as someone kicked him firmly in the rear.

A little man—he couldn't have been more than four feet tall—started cackling. "Consider yourself big-people-bashed, sucker!" Skeeter lunged for him, but the kicker ran off, laughing all the way.

Skeeter puckered his lips, hoping he would still get his kiss. But the moment was ruined. Violet clicked her key chain, and her car beeped loudly.

A bright, shiny, new red sports car.

"Oh, wow!" Skeeter gasped. "So *that*'s how I'm getting it."

"Getting what?" Violet asked.

"You know. The car." Skeeter figured he should try to act a little humble, at least at first. That's what a gentleman would do, right? "I really shouldn't. I couldn't."

Violet giggled. "My car? Whatever are you talking about, Skeeter?"

"I'm talking about a very, very generous young lady, who is going to give her rescuer a cherry red sports car. For freeeeeeee!"

Violet took a step back. "Um, I'm leaving."

She climbed into the car, while Skeeter just stood on the side of the road. "Uh, do you have some *other* car at home that you want to give me?" he asked.

Violet drove away without answering. Skeeter stood there for several long minutes, waiting.

Nothing happened.

He truly didn't get it. "So, seriously?" he asked, looking around at the empty street. "No sports car?"

Chapter Nine

The next morning, bright and early, there was a knock at the cabana door.

"Hello?" Jill poked her head into the room.

"Hey, Aunt Jill." Bobbi and Patrick waved fries at her.

"Hey, guys." Jill pulled up a seat at the table. "So, how'd it go last night?" Skeeter didn't look up from the papers he'd spread out across the table. He was trying to come up with a good idea for the new hotel. "A dwarf kicked my butt, and I didn't get a free sports car."

"He's talking about our bedtime story last night," Bobbi explained.

"Uncle Skeeter said Jeremiah would get a new horse and a kiss from the fair lady," Patrick added, "but I said a dwarf would kick his butt."

Skeeter looked up. A lightning bolt of an idea crackled across his mind. "*You* said it," he said, staring at Patrick. "Maybe *that's* how it works. . . ."

"Okay, time to go to school," Jill said.

"Why don't we be cool to these kids today and not make them go to school?" Skeeter suggested. If they stayed home, they could tell another story. . . .

"What?" Bobbi asked in alarm. "I don't want to miss school."

"Yeah, school's gonna be awesome today," Patrick agreed.

Skeeter was shocked. "Wow, I never heard a kid say that."

"You would if that kid went to *our* school," Jill informed him.

The kids gathered their stuff and bustled out the door. As they went, Skeeter could hear Patrick talking to Jill. "We helped Uncle Skeeter with his hotel ideas this morning!"

And you'll be helping me even more tonight, Skeeter thought.

As he was about to close the door behind them, Kendall appeared in the doorway. "You need something?" Skeeter asked, hoping the answer was no.

"I know you feel you need to prepare for our big 'showdown,' but that doesn't excuse you from your maintenance responsibilities," Kendall said, using his prissiest manager voice. "There are lights out in the spa, the south service elevator's running slow, and the lock on the kitchen freezer is broken."

Skeeter sighed. "I'll get right on it . . . sir."

"Darn right you will." Kendall leaned closer to Skeeter and lowered his voice. "I heard about your hero act with my girlfriend last night," he murmured in a warning tone. "I know what you're trying to do, and it ain't gonna work. You're gonna have to find a different way to cozy up to the old man, 'cause Violet Nottingham's not gonna date a gum-scraping handyman."

Skeeter clenched his fists. He was much more than a handyman. *So* much more. "You know, Kendall, I'm considering keeping you on when I get the general manager job," Skeeter told him, "so you better watch your tone with me."

Kendall snorted. "Your brief trip to the land of make-believe is just about over, Bronson. Your dad ran this hotel into the ground. Fortunately, you're not gonna get the chance to do it again."

After the encounter with Kendall, Skeeter fumed for the rest of the day. He would have been even more upset if he'd known where Kendall went next. Kendall was supposed to meet Mr. Nottingham's work crew at the new hotel site, but when he followed the directions he'd been given, he found himself outside a small, cheery-looking schoolhouse. He called back to the Nottingham headquarters for confirmation. And he got it. "Really?" Kendall said into the phone, surprised that Barry Nottingham would want to tear down a school to build his hotel. "Here? That's—" He broke off as he spotted two familiar-looking kids eating lunch outside.

Suddenly, Kendall realized who they were: Bobbi and Patrick, the kids who'd been following Skeeter around all week long. A broad smile spread across Kendall's face. "That's fantastic," he told the guy on the other end of the phone. Barry Nottingham couldn't have picked a better site.

Chapter
Ten

Skeeter couldn't wait for bedtime. The day felt like it stretched on forever, but finally the sun set.

When Jill showed up with the kids, Skeeter guided the group in a different direction. Instead of going straight to his room, he led them to the elevator. They took it up as high as it would go. The doors opened on a blazing pink sky. Skeeter led them out onto the roof, showing off the 360-degree view of the city. Even Jill was impressed.

To the east, mountains poked through the smog,

towering over the city lights. In the west, if you squinted, you could almost see the sparkling blue of the ocean. The sky dimmed as the sun set below the horizon and the city twinkled even brighter.

Skeeter had another surprise in store. He lit a little campfire, then whipped out a big bag of marshmallows. Soon the four of them were happily stuffing their faces with warm, bubbly s'mores.

"I heard about marshmallows, saw them in magazines, but never imagined they'd be this good," Patrick mumbled around a mouthful of sugary goodness. "They're smooshy, they're sticky, they rock my world. I wish I was a marshmallow, 'cause I'd eat myself every day."

"I just hope your mother doesn't find out I gave you some," Skeeter said.

"I won't tell her," Patrick promised. "I swear."

"I'm not worried about you," Skeeter said. He nodded toward Jill. "She's the weak link."

Jill suppressed a smile. "I think I can look the other way on this one."

Skeeter nodded in appreciation. "All right, the mermaid's being cool."

"The what?" Jill asked, looking confused.

"Nothing." Skeeter and Patrick exchanged a glance, then burst into laughter.

Bobbi sighed and stared up at the sky. "Look how bright the stars are tonight."

"They are beautiful from up here," Jill agreed.

Skeeter looked up. The moon had disappeared behind a cloud, darkening the sky. The stars blazed. He tried to count the twinkling lights, but there were too many.

"When I was growing up, me and your mom used to lay on the roof of our motel at night with my old man—your grandpa—and we'd see if we could spot things in the stars." Skeeter pointed to a cluster of lights directly overhead. "Like, see those stars over there? That looks like a camel to me."

"Look right next to the moon," Jill said, pointing at the stars. "It looks exactly like Bugsy." As they all burst into laughter, Skeeter couldn't help but notice how pretty Jill was. Her skin was almost glowing in the starlight.

"Uncle Skeeter?" Bobbi's voice was quieter than usual.

"Yeah, pal?"

"Do you think my father will come back?"

Skeeter paused, trying to come up with the perfect thing to say. But he'd never been very good at saying the perfect thing. So he decided to go with what was in his heart. "I wish I knew," he admitted. "He must be going through some major mental malfunction to stay away from you guys this long. But I know if he were here, and he was in his right mind, he would be mighty proud of how brave you've been with all this."

"Brave?" Bobbi asked, like she wasn't sure she should let herself believe it. "Really?"

"Heck, yeah," Skeeter said. "Braver than any of these heroes I've been talking about."

Bobbi smiled proudly, and Jill gave Skeeter a surprised look, like maybe he wasn't the person she'd expected. Then she gave herself a little shake. "Okay, you guys made me late," Jill said, in a businesslike tone. "I hope you're happy." She stood up, waving good-bye to Skeeter. "The kids told me you have some big presentation or something this weekend. If you need extra time to prepare, I can try to get off work early tomorrow."

"I'm good," Skeeter assured her. "I've been thinking about what makes a great hotel since I was six—I'll be ready."

"You sure?" Jill asked. "Because I can—"

"Hey, I got it, I'm good," Skeeter said. "I'm going to win. Thanks, anyway."

"Oh." Jill rolled her eyes. "How wonderful for you. See you in the morning. Bye, kids."

"All right," Skeeter announced, as soon as the elevator doors closed behind Jill. "Now we can get down to business. I have a great story for tonight: the Great Hotel Idea War."

Patrick and Bobbi didn't look particularly impressed by the idea.

"Come on," Skeeter wheedled. "I need to tell this one. It'll be real exciting, I swear."

Patrick and Bobbi just stared at him. Skeeter sighed. "Fine. We can put it off one more night, I guess," he said, promising himself not to let it go any longer than that. "But what do you want to hear?"

"How about some Evel Knievel stuff," Patrick said excitedly. "Racing, jumping, flying, crashing!"

"Or maybe some, like . . ." Bobbi blushed. "Romantic stuff?"

Skeeter raised his eyebrows. "Oh, you want a little romance, do you?" he teased. "I can go for that. How about I do one with a little action *and* a little romance?" Skeeter thought for a moment, and soon the perfect idea popped into his head. He began the story.

The greatest of all the heroes of Ancient Greece was, of course, Skeetacus. He was only a peasant, but he was a fierce warrior, a soulful poet, and a wicked good chariot driver.

"How good?" Patrick asked.

"Let's put it this way," Skeeter said. "You know how Hercules supposedly founded the

Olympics? Well, Skeetacus invented the X-Games."

"Can we get to the romance now?" Bobbi requested.

"Why not?" Skeeter agreed. "Who is Skeetacus's lucky girl?"

"In these stories it's always the fairest maiden in the land," Bobbi pointed out.

"Do *you* think a lowly, gum-scraping peasant has a shot with the fairest maiden in all the land?" Skeeter asked his niece.

She looked at him like he was crazy for even asking. "Of course!"

Yes! Skeeter thought. Bobbi said it, not me. Maybe this time, it would actually work. "So where do they go?" he prodded. "Maybe they get thirsty? Can they get a drink?"

"Yeah, they could go to an old tavern," Bobbi said. And she picked up the story herself.

Skeetacus and his date stumbled upon a small tavern. Inside, they discovered all the girls who were mean to Skeetacus growing up.

"Hey! No girls were ever mean to Skeetacus

growing up!" Skeeter protested. "All right . . . a few girls were mean to Skeetacus." He paused, then just spit out the truth. "Fine, a lot of girls were mean to Skeetacus. Good. Good. Go."

They see he is now with the fairest maiden in all the land, and they are really jealous. They're so jealous that they don't even know what to do. They just start nervously doing the hokey-pokey.

So then Skeetacus takes his date out to walk on the beach.

"Oh, so the date's at the beach!" Skeeter said eagerly. "Bathing-suit time!"

Patrick and Bobbi continued the story, each of them tossing out ideas as soon as they popped into their heads.

All of a sudden, a big hairy guy washes up on the shore, passed out. Skeetacus runs over and steps on the guy's stomach, making him spit out water and a fish. He starts breathing normally again. Then it starts pouring! So they run into a magical cave! And Abe Lincoln is there!

"Hey, is this a joke to you?" Skeeter asked, sounding annoyed.

The kids recoiled from the tension in his voice. Skeeter realized he had gone too far. "I mean, I'm sorry," he said quickly. "The Abe Lincoln thing is fine. I just . . . he gets to kiss her, right? Yes? No? Anybody?" But the kids just stared at him.

Skeeter decided that no answer was the best answer he was going to get.

He turned out the light and put himself to bed. When he finally fell asleep that night, he dreamed of the perfect kiss.

Chapter Eleven

The next day, Skeeter drove out to the coast. He strolled along the boardwalk enjoying the warm sea breeze. The sun was shining, the sky was clear—it was the perfect weather for a day at the beach.

Skeeter had Violet Nottingham's number programmed into his cell phone's speed dial. Just in case he needed it.

He needed it.

"Hello?" she said, her voice as lovely and polished as always.

"Is this the fairest maiden in the land?" Skeeter asked, trying not to sound nervous.

"Skeeter Bronson, is that you?" Violet asked.

"I'm down at the beach, and I bet you're in the mood for a little lunch."

"That sounds so delightful," Violet said.

Yes! he thought. Everything was going the way it was supposed to.

"But—"

But? There was no *but* in the story.

"I'm afraid I'm on my way to Vegas for the day," Violet said.

"Vegas?" Skeeter couldn't believe it. "Right now?"

"Don't tell Kendall. He thinks I'm in the library."

"Wow." It wasn't supposed to happen this way. "I, uh . . . really thought we were gonna see each other today."

"I'll see you at Daddy's birthday party," Violet reminded him. "Look, I have to run; doing an interview with *French Vogue* on the other line." She hung up before Skeeter had a chance to say good-bye.

Skeeter told himself not to worry. They would still have their date—it was meant to be. It just wasn't meant to be today. Walking with his head down, he headed for a bench along the ocean. As he was crossing the boardwalk, an in-line skater slammed into him. They both tumbled to the ground.

When Skeeter untangled himself and dusted himself off, he finally looked up at the skater. It was Jill!

"Oh, I'm so sorry!" she exclaimed, helping him to his feet. "Are you okay?"

"Yeah, yeah. Fine," Skeeter said, even though he was feeling bruised all over. "I wasn't looking. What are you doing here, anyway? Shouldn't you be at school?"

"This is my lunch period," she explained.

"I'm supposed to be looking for a job right now, but for some reason, I felt like coming to the beach today. You hungry?"

"Me?" Skeeter asked, surprised that Jill would want to spend any time with him voluntarily. "Yeah. I could eat."

"Well, I'm buying," Jill said. "This way it's kind of like a settlement for our accident, and you can't sue me."

"Somebody stole my wallet anyway," Skeeter said. "So . . . deal."

They found a cozy-looking tavern along the shore. It was almost empty inside, but a group of women were gathered around a table in the far corner.

"Oh, my gosh!" one of them blurted out at the sight of Skeeter. "Is that Skeeter Bronson?"

With a knowing smile, he turned around to face the woman. She was an old enemy.

"Remember me, Skeeter?" the woman asked. "Donna Hynde? From high school?"

"Of course." He remembered her all right.

Just like he remembered every nasty thing she'd ever said to him. "Hello, Donna."

"This is so funny!" Donna gushed. "We're sitting here planning our twenty-five-year reunion! You remember these guys, right? Rose? Julia? Mary?"

"Hello, ladies." Back in high school, Skeeter had asked every single one of them out on a date—and every single one had laughed in his face. "Nice to see you again." And it was—but only because he knew what was going to happen next. "This is Jill."

Jill gave them a small wave. Skeeter leaned toward her. "Will you pretend to be my girlfriend right now?" he whispered. "I'll explain later."

"I'm not comfortable with that," she muttered through gritted teeth.

"I'll make you some more s'mores," Skeeter said, hoping the bribe would work.

Jill groaned, but how could she turn down an offer like that. "Okay." Jill nodded. "I'll do it."

Skeeter cleared his throat. "Ladies, I'd like you to meet Jill," he said, "my girlfriend."

He looked pointedly at Jill, waiting. She rolled her eyes at him, but then grabbed his arm. "Oh, Skeeter," she simpered, "you're the best boyfriend ever. So romantic. And . . . great." She stopped to think for a second. "Life is good," she added, nodding and squeezing Skeeter a little tighter. "Life is really good."

Mary's eyes widened. "You are *so* pretty," she told Jill.

Jill smiled. "Thank you."

"You know," Donna said, "we were kind of mean to Skeeter back in school."

"Skeeter?" Jill asked in disbelief. "*My* Skeeter?"

"Yeah," Donna said, looking sheepish. "We feel kind of bad about it now."

"Nobody deserves to have an ant farm dumped down their pants," Rose said.

"Or to have their diary read over the loud-speaker," Mary added.

"Or to be voted most likely to have pimples the rest of his life," Donna finished.

Skeeter cringed at the memories.

Donna watched his face and then dug in her purse for a second. She pulled out a business card and handed it to Skeeter. "If I can ever do anything to make it up to you, please let me know."

"Yeah. And you turned out . . . pretty cute," Julia admitted.

Soon they were all talking at once, spitting out the compliments as fast as they could come up with them.

"And you have a beautiful girlfriend."

"You obviously work out."

One of the women extended her right hand.

Wait a second. That was strange. That was actually *really* odd. Then Skeeter remembered how the bedtime story had ended. And he smiled.

It got even odder when Mary quickly jerked her right hand behind her. She looked like she didn't understand why her arm was moving like that.

Skeeter shook his head in amusement. "I love Patrick's imagination," he said.

"Me, too," Jill agreed, though she had no idea what that had to do with anything.

A moment later, the women all broke into song and began turning themselves around.

"You want to hokeypokey on out of here?" Skeeter asked Jill.

She was out the door before he finished the sentence. Skeeter followed, and they decided to wander back toward the beach.

"So I spoke to Wendy," Jill said, breaking the silence between them.

"Oh, yeah? She okay?" Skeeter asked.

"Yeah," Jill said. "Just waiting for good news from a couple of schools. She can't wait to see the kids tomorrow. She's never been away from them this long."

Skeeter stopped in his tracks. He'd forgotten she was coming back so soon. "Wow . . . yeah," he said slowly. After today, everything would go back to normal. No more kids. No more stories. "Tomorrow."

"They're gonna be devastated," Jill told him. "They worship you and those amazing bedtime stories you tell them."

"They come up with all the good parts," Skeeter said fondly. "Believe me."

Jill gasped as a fat, hairy man washed up on the beach. "Oh, no!" she cried, rushing over to the man. "Is he unconscious?"

"Have no fear," Skeeter said confidently. He knew exactly what he was supposed to do. "Skeetacus is here." He jumped down hard on the man's chest. The man sputtered. A gush of water—and a *fish*—popped out of his mouth. His eyes flew open. "Thanks!" he exclaimed, sucking in deep breaths of air.

"No problemicus," Skeeter said cheerfully.

Once they'd made sure the guy was all right, they walked on down the shore. Jill looked at Skeeter as if she didn't even recognize him. "Check out Mr. Smooth," she said wonderingly.

Skeeter shrugged it off. "Well, you know, I do what I do. We should get out of this rain."

Jill looked up at the cloudless sky. "What rain?" But as the words came out of her mouth, she felt the first patter on her forehead. There was a second drop, then a third, and then the skies opened up. The water came down in sheets. Seconds later, they were drenched.

"Over there!" Jill pointed toward a covered area beneath the boardwalk, and the two of them raced for shelter. They ducked into a dank, gloomy space beneath the aging boardwalk.

They watched the rain pound the sand. "Tomorrow's the big presentation, huh?" Jill asked. "I know you're not worried, but good luck on it anyway."

"Thanks." Suddenly, Skeeter had an idea. "Hey, you want to come? It's actually a party, and Wendy should be home by then to watch the kids."

Jill raised her eyebrows. "Are you asking me out on a date?"

"Well . . ." Skeeter gave her a sheepish grin. "Actually, isn't *this* kind of a date?"

"You wish." Jill's cheeks flushed red with embarrassment. "Okay, I'll meet you there after my night class."

A blast of thunder splintered the silence, and Jill flinched, inching closer to Skeeter. Getting soaked in the rain on the beach had made her look even prettier.

"Wow," Skeeter said, staring at Jill. "I just realized something."

"Yeah?" She brushed the rainwater out of her sparkling eyes.

Even with wet hair and mascara running down her face, she was still beautiful. Skeeter couldn't believe he'd been so blind. "You're the fairest maiden in the land."

"Me?" Jill asked, confused. "You mean 'fair' like 'doesn't cheat at checkers'? 'Cause I'm very fair like that."

"No." Skeeter drew closer. "Fair as in . . . beautiful." He felt a charge in the air—like if he touched her, there might be sparks. And if he kissed her . . .

That's when he remembered the story. Specifically, he remembered what came next.

"I think something weird's about to happen," Skeeter said, looking around nervously.

Jill flinched and backed away. "Yeah, this is a mistake. I don't know what I was thinking."

"No!" Skeeter protested. "I meant—" But before he could finish, the boardwalk over their heads began to shake. Heavy footsteps rattled the wooden planks.

BOOM! BOOM! BOOM!

"Oh, no!" Skeeter tensed. "Here comes Abe!"

As a runner passed overhead, something clinked against the wood and then slipped through a crack between the planks and plopped into the sand. Skeeter picked up the slim, shiny, orange object.

"A penny!" He examined the bearded face carved into the copper. "The Abe Lincoln part is over! We're good now!"

Skeeter was all ready to get back to the gazing-into-each-others'-eyes thing. But Jill was over it.

"Yeah, wow, a penny," she said in disgust. "How about we just get going?" The rain stopped abruptly, and she walked off.

Skeeter looked up at the sky in exasperation. "Great imagination, Patrick!"

Chapter Twelve

That night, Bobbi and Patrick weren't in the mood to go to bed. Maybe because Skeeter had fed them a pile of candy bars for dinner. Now they were on a sugar high. But they stayed quiet for as long as they could, and Skeeter began a new story. He knew this was it, his one big chance to make sure that everything went right with his presentation for Mr. Nottingham. His entire life—and his life's dream—depended on getting this story right. (So maybe he shouldn't have stuffed the kids with quite so much sugar.)

"The fate of the entire universe hung in the balance," Skeeter began . . .

. . . *as the Supreme Galactic Council met to determine who would control the new planet in the vast Nottinghamian star system.*

The Supreme Leader Baracto sat on his large throne, looking out at the stars. To his right sat the Countess Vio. To his left, General Kendallo, the evil governor of Hotellium, awaited the Supreme Leader's decision. The room was crowded with aliens. Most in attendance expected Baracto to rule in favor of General Kendallo. But before he could do so, the door to the royal chamber whooshed open, revealing Skeeto Bronsonion, the fastest space pilot this side of the Milky Way. His faithful sidekick, Lieutenant Mik, followed closely behind.

Skeeto swaggered into the room as if he owned it. "All right, all you androids and andrettes," Skeeto said smoothly, "let's get this shindig started—my star cruiser is double-parked."

"He shouldn't talk like that!" Bobbi cut in suddenly.

"Yeah, Skeeto sounds a little too big-shotty," Patrick said. "That's how Kendallo should talk. Skeeto should sound more like a goofy alien. More like . . ."

"M'tao gar-gar hee-so!" Skeeto said angrily. *"Shneesh zap plok!"*

"What?" Skeeter said, dismayed. "He's gotta sound like that the whole time?"

Bobbi and Patrick, still on a sugar high, smacked hands in triumphant glee. "Yes!"

"Silence!" Baracto boomed at the babbling pilot. "It is time to present the theme of our new planet. But first—has everyone washed their hands?"

Everyone in the room nodded yes, even those aliens who didn't have any hands.

"Excellent," approved the Supreme Leader. "General Kendallo, you may begin."

General Kendallo stepped forward. "With

pleasure, your magnificence," he said, sucking up with every word. (It was, after all, what he did best.) "If I was given control of the new planet, I would make the first rule: inhabitants will not be allowed to communicate with speech. They will only communicate through . . . soooooooong!"

"Blef sa croso grax!" Skeeto cut in, sounding infuriated. "Ee-schnarf-nay! Z'tai borf! Shleef nagi-nagi floobu!"

The faithful Lieutenant Mik translated for him. "Ambassador Skeeto feels this is the most ridiculous thing he has ever heard. He feels his plan for the new planet is the only way to go!"

"With all due respect," General Kendallo said, sounding not very respectful at all, "Ambassador Skeeto is not fit to lead a Forellian space gorilla farm, let alone a star system. This was proven by the failure of his father before him."

Skeeto couldn't let a comment like that pass. He let loose a stream of furious alien talk . . . which, unfortunately, no one understood.

Once again, Mik translated for the crowd. "If

you want to talk about my father, maybe we should talk about your mother," he said. "He says your mother is so ugly, she could put her face in dough and make Captain Bugzoid cookies."

Captain Bugzoid, a giant hamsterlike alien, looked up in confusion. "Huh?"

"Ha plash tad a do," Skeeto told him.

"He says, no offense Captain Bugzoid," Mik explained.

"Enough!" Supreme Lord Baracto snapped. "We will settle this the old-fashioned way. A no-gravity fight."

Once everyone but Skeeto and Kendallo had strapped on their gravity belts, Baracto reached over and flipped the switch marked GRAVITY. Kendallo and Skeeto floated several feet in the air. They flailed wildly, reaching out for each other, but with nothing to push off against, it was no use. They were just swimming in space, going nowhere.

Kendallo pulled out a ray gun and aimed it at Skeeto. He pulled the trigger.

A laser hand popped out of the gun and slapped Skeeto's face.

A kid-shaped android tossed Skeeto a ray gun of his own. He fired.

A laser fist popped out and punched Kendallo in the face. Kendallo shot again, then Skeeto, and the laser fists punched, poked, pinched, pulled, and punched some more.

"This is boring," Countess Vio complained.

"I quite agree," Baracto said. He gestured to one of his attendants. "Bring out the Glopozoid!"

The crowd gasped. A door midway up the wall slid open, and a hideous orange monster slithered out. The glopozoid had eight arms, crossed eyes, an ugly drooling mouth, and a fish-like tail that enabled it to swim easily and swifly through the air. It chuffed and grunted as it sailed across the room, heading straight for Skeeto.

The Glopozoid swarmed over Skeeto and threw him into the wall. Then it veered in the opposite direction, chasing after Kendallo. After bouncing him off the wall a few times, the

Glopozoid licked Kendallo's head with a loud, slobbery slurp.

"Ashooby-snarf!" Skeeto shouted as Kendallo screeched in terror.

The Glopozoid snarled, revealing rows of razor-sharp teeth. Skeeter didn't even flinch. He aimed a steely glance at the monster. "Sa-soo geebar, zaza," he said in a steady voice.

Skeeto launched himself toward the gravity switch, then slammed his palm into it and hung on tight. The Glopozoid slammed into the floor and smashed to bits.

Baracto and Countess Vio descended from their thrones and made their way down to Skeeto, who was gently lowering himself to the ground.

"Arise, Skeeto," Baracto intoned. "Ruler of Nottinghamia!"

Skeeto raised his hands in triumph. "Noshnar yeet-yo gotay! Gotay! Gotay!"

Skeeter thought he was going to explode with happiness. He felt like he'd already won in the real world, not just in the story. And he knew it was only a matter of time. "Kids, you did it," Skeeter said. "That was the perfect ending for our last story."

"Oh, that's not the end," Patrick said.

"Yeah, that would be too obvious," Bobbi added.

"Somebody threw a fireball at Skeeto," Patrick said, bursting with excitement. "And Skeeto got incineratated."

Bobbi pumped her fist in the air. "Yes!"

As the kids collapsed in laughter, Skeeter felt as if his head were on fire. "Incineratated? You mean, incinerated? Noooooo!" he pleaded. "Don't say that!"

Patrick started rolling around on the floor. "I'm Skeeto!" he cackled. "I'm burning up!"

"And all that was left of Skeeto was a pile of ashes!" Bobbi sputtered, in between loud giggles. "The end!"

Skeeter couldn't breathe. He felt like the Glopozoid was sitting on his chest. "The story can't end like that," he gasped. "Where's the happy ending?"

"You told us happy endings don't really happen," Bobbi reminded him. "We want our story to be real."

"Wait, you guys are making me catch *fire*," Skeeter quickly pointed out. They wanted *that* to be real? "I still win, right? How could I win if I'm incineratated?"

The kids lay down and pulled up the covers, but Skeeter grabbed hold of the blankets and tugged them down again. "You can't sleep until you change that ending!" he shouted. "Once you fall asleep, the story is locked! How'd you like it if I did this to you, huh? How would you like that?"

He was interrupted by a knock at the door.

"Skeeter?" an old woman's voice called. Skeeter recognized it as Mrs. Dixon, the guest who believed in leprechauns. "Are you all right in there?"

"Yes, Mrs. Dixon!" Skeeter called back.

"I don't believe you," Mrs. Dixon said. "I'm calling 5-1-1."

Skeeter told himself to calm down. He hurried over to the door, opened it, and forced a smile. "I'm not sure what '5-1-1' is, but I'm really fine, Mrs. Dixon, I promise you. I raised my voice, but in a *fun* way. Thank you for your concern."

"I called the front desk to fix my shower, and the troll lady told me to have the leprechaun fix it," she complained. "But I'm not on good terms with him right now."

Skeeter tried not to let his irritation show. It wasn't her fault she was interrupting him at a moment of crisis. "I'll be done in a minute," he said. "Okay, Mrs. Dixon?"

"All right." She gave him a kindly smile. "Good night, Skeeter."

He rushed back to the bedroom—but he was too late. Bobbi and Patrick were already asleep. Which meant Skeeter couldn't change the story.

Skeeter was afraid that for him, this was the end. (And not the happily-ever-after kind.)

Chapter Thirteen

Mr. Nottingham's birthday party was the biggest social event of the season. And Skeeter was determined to make a good impression.

He was also determined not to get incinerated.

So on his way, he made a last-minute stop at the hardware store. He rolled his cart up the aisle, grabbing every bottle of sunscreen he could find. Then he tossed in a few smoke detectors and an armful of oven mitts. It seemed like protection enough—and then he spotted the big bottle of flame-resistant tree spray.

"Makes your Christmas tree fire retardant!" it advertised.

Skeeter sprayed some on his wrist. He took a big sniff.

Pine fresh!

And if it was good enough for a Christmas tree, it was good enough for him. He sprayed it all over himself. Twice. *Now* he was ready to go to the party.

Skeeter thought he was totally covered—but there was one thing he hadn't prepared for: Kendall. Skeeter had no idea just how devious Kendall could be. While Skeeter was busy shopping for fire-protection supplies, Kendall was running an errand of his own. He'd tracked down Jill at her school and told her the truth about where the new hotel was going to be built.

Or, at least, he told her *his* version of the truth.

"I just thought you should know," Kendall

told her, trying his best to sound apologetic. "I can't believe he didn't tell you. I mean, I'm sure it's just a coincidence that the hotel's going up on the site of your school—well, pretty sure . . ."

Kendall could tell from the look on Jill's face that he didn't have to say anything more. Jill's imagination would do the job for him.

And as Skeeter drove to the party, eager to make his presentation (and even more eager to have his date with Jill), he had no idea that his entire world was about to come crashing down around him.

"Disco Inferno," one of Skeeter's favorite songs, came on the radio. He began singing along, until he realized what he was singing. Inferno—as in, storm of fire. As in, incinerated.

He changed the station. Which was kind of difficult, given that he was wearing oven mitts. But he managed.

Madonna started singing her '80s hit, "Burning Up."

Skeeter groaned and switched stations.

The Bangles' "Eternal Flame."

The next station: Bruce Springsteen rocking out to "I'm on Fire."

Skeeter turned off the radio.

Mr. Nottingham's house was big enough to be a Nottingham hotel. There were tennis courts, two pools, a private movie theater, a marble fountain—and rumor had it that the basement housed a secret bowling alley. Mr. Nottingham gave Skeeter the grand tour, boasting about his new hotel every step of the way. But Skeeter barely heard him. The house was filled with flames: the open grill sizzling with shrimp. The roaring fireplace. The glowing red tip of Mr. Nottingham's cigar. The menorah with candles blazing. Skeeter moaned and hurried away.

He quickly grabbed himself an ice cream—which seemed safe enough—and joined Mickey on the other side of the room. "Have you seen Jill?" he asked, scanning the area. "She should have been here by now."

"No, haven't seen her," Mickey replied.

Skeeter was searching for Jill so intently that he didn't notice the large bumblebee that had landed on top of his ice cream. At least he didn't notice until he took a giant bite—and nearly swallowed the bee.

"*Ow!*" Skeeter yelped. He jumped up and down, trying to spit out the bee. But it was too busy buzzing and stinging to go anywhere.

"What happened?" Mickey asked, watching his friend have some kind of fit.

"A bee . . . on my ice cream . . . stung my tongue . . ." Skeeter said, or tried to say. His tongue was already swelling so much that the words were incomprehensible.

The room fell silent as Aspen struck a giant gong. "The meeting on the new hotel will take place in the living room," she announced.

Skeeter hesitated outside the living room, knowing that his destiny lay within. He drew in a deep breath, wincing at his painful tongue—then stepped inside.

Violet Nottingham, Mickey, and Aspen sat around a huge oak conference table. Behind them, the room was crowded with hotel employees. Mr. Nottingham himself sat at the head of the table, looking like a king.

"Happy birthday, Mr. Nottingham," Kendall said heartily, entering behind Skeeter.

"Thank you, Kendall," Mr. Nottingham said. "As you can see, I invited some of the staff to sit in, to see how your ideas will play with 'the regular folk.'" He glanced at the maids and room-service waiters sitting behind him. "No offense."

"None taken, Barry," Mickey said, speaking for all his coworkers.

"*Mr. Nottingham,*" the big boss corrected him. He cleared his throat. "Gentlemen. Who would like to go first?"

Skeeter slapped a hand over his mouth and pointed at Kendall. His tongue still hurt too much to speak.

Kendall stepped forward, confident as ever. "I

would, sir." He blew a kiss to Violet, who batted her eyes.

"Mr. Nottingham, you were absolutely right about the 'rock and roll' theme being old hat," Kendall said in an oily voice. "Your insight inspired me to dig deeper, to find the commonality at the heart of the American experience."

Skeeter was disgusted. Nottingham couldn't actually be buying this, could he? But one look at Nottingham made it clear: he was.

"It was in the midst of this analysis—inspired, as it was, by your wisdom," Kendall continued, oozing smarm, "that I had probably the greatest idea I've ever had in my whole life. To build a hotel that celebrates one of the pillars of this country's cultural heritage, an artistic legacy that is uniquely American. I speak, of course, of the musical theater, and, more specifically—" He pulled out a top hat and placed it on his head. "—of the Great White Way."

The audience jerked in surprise.

Kendall started singing, then added a jaunty

kick-step. "'Come on along and listen to, the lullaby of Broadway.'" His voice sounded like a cat howling from inside a rusty kettle. "'The hip-hooray and bally-hoo, the lullaby of Broadway.'"

Even Violet looked embarrassed for her boyfriend. (Or maybe just for herself.)

Soon—though not soon enough—Kendall stopped singing. He brought out a detailed model of the new hotel, pointing to different features as he spoke. "And so we have the 'Some Enchanted Evening' nightclub, the 'My Favorite Things' shopping concourse, the *Grease* hair salon, the twin swimming pools—one for the Sharks, one for the Jets, the Tony Award Terrace, and 400 dedicated staff members—all dressed like cats." Kendall beamed as if he'd just won a Tony award of his own. "What can I say, except—" He burst into song again. "'I dreamed the impossible dream!'"

Everyone looked vaguely ill, including Mr. Nottingham.

"That was . . . impressive," he said weakly. He turned to Skeeter. "You're up."

His heart pounding, Skeeter took his place at the head of the room. He didn't have any charts or props. He didn't have Kendall's polished way of talking or a choreographed dance routine—and he definitely didn't have a top hat. All he had were his dreams and his one big idea. But something told him that just this once that would be enough.

"Ibe dug rinkid ow bis," Skeeter stopped. He realized that no one could understand what he was saying with his bee-stung tongue.

"Are you all right, Skeeter?" Mr. Nottingham asked.

"Ub dee bunked by unh." He was starting to panic. "Ub *dee . . . bunked . . .* by *unh*."

The room was silent. And then Mickey popped out of his seat. "A bee stung my tongue," he said.

Mr. Nottingham looked at him in surprise. "You understand him?" He glanced at Skeeter. "How did a bee sting your tongue?"

"Ib dub bom by eye beem bo," Skeeter said.

"It was on his ice-cream cone," Mickey said, translating.

"Wow." Barry chuckled. "Sounds like that cone had a little sting to it."

Kendall laughed heartily. Once a suck-up, always a suck-up.

"Can you translate Skeeter's presentation for us?" Mr. Nottingham asked.

"I'll give it a go," Mickey said.

Skeeter sighed with relief. Maybe this would work after all. It *had* to, right? Just like it said in the story.

"Ibe dug rinkid ow bis," Skeeter began, speaking from his heart.

Mickey translated every word of it. "I spent the last week in a hotel, the hotel where I live, with my niece and nephew. Seeing it through their eyes reminded me of my own childhood, when I had the privilege of growing up in a motel. To a kid, everything about a hotel is strange and wonderful: sleeping in a different bed, hanging out in the lobby, riding the elevator. Some hotels try to make it seem as much like home as they can. But they're missing the point: if you wanted to stay in a place like home, why not just stay home? Our guests should experience an escape from the everyday, an adventure, and that's what I'd like to capture in the new hotel. What every kid knows, and every adult forgets: it's fun to try new things."

When Mickey finished speaking, tears welling in his eyes, the audience froze, waiting for Mr. Nottingham's reaction.

"That . . . is *brilliant*," he said, which was as enthusiastic as Barry ever got. He stood and smiled. "Congratulations, you've just won the keys to the kingdom, my boy."

Skeeter couldn't believe it. He'd never been so happy in his entire life. After all this time, his dream had finally come true.

As the meeting broke up, everyone came over to congratulate him—even Kendall.

"You deserve it, pal," he said, with a weirdly

satisfied smile. "You've got an iron will. I wouldn't have the guts to knock down the school where my niece and nephew went, where my sister was principal, where my girlfriend taught . . . because that's where the hotel's being built!"

Skeeter stared blankly. What was Kendall talking about? But before he could find out, Violet stepped before the group. "Time for Daddy's birthday cake!" she announced. Her accent was still lovely, but Skeeter barely noticed anymore. Violet may have been pretty, but she was nothing compared to how Skeeter saw Jill. "Everybody outside."

"Good show, son," Mr. Nottingham told Skeeter on his way out. "The bee-sting language was really working for ya on a sympathetic level."

"Sir, I really need to speak with you for a second," Skeeter said, relieved that the swelling in his tongue seemed to be going down, and he could finally talk again.

But his words were drowned out by the crowd, as they launched into a chorus of "Happy

Birthday." A team of hula girls carried out a massive birthday cake.

Skeeter didn't see the cake. He only saw a flickering orange maw of flame—the cake was made to look like a Hawaiian volcano surrounded by hundreds of candles. It was like a slow-motion fireball, and it was heading straight for him. A squad of fire dancers followed behind, spinning fiery torches. The flames danced and licked at the air, reaching for Skeeter.

There was nowhere to run.

There was nowhere to hide.

Good thing he'd brought along his lucky portable fire extinguisher. Skeeter sprayed the volcano. He sprayed the cake. He sprayed the chefs. He even sprayed Mr. Nottingham. By the time he was done, everyone and everything in sight was covered in foam. Mr. Nottingham wiped his face clear and aimed his laserlike glare at Skeeter.

"Bronson!" he shouted, his cheeks turning red beneath the foam, "you're *fired*!"

Chapter Fourteen

The next morning, Skeeter tracked down Jill at school. He found her in the hallway, just outside her classroom. As soon as she spotted him, she turned away.

"Go away, Skeeter," she said harshly.

"Why won't you pick up the phone?" Skeeter asked.

She kept her back to him. "Because I know it's you calling."

Skeeter had to make her understand. This

wasn't his fault. "Look, you gotta believe me, I had no idea—"

Jill's voice was muffled, like she was choking back her emotion—or her tears. "Skeeter, don't destroy the sliver of respect I still have for you by making lame excuses. Just go away. And stay away."

She disappeared inside her classroom. Skeeter took a step toward the door—then stopped. There was no point, he realized. She would never believe him. Not unless he found a way to prove himself to her. So instead he walked away.

And straight into Bobbi and Patrick.

Skeeter didn't want to face the look in their eyes. But he forced himself not to turn away.

"Did you incineratate our school because we incineratated you in the story?" Patrick asked.

Skeeter couldn't believe Patrick could think that. "No, of course not."

"We thought you were always supposed to be the good guy," Bobbi said, disappointed.

"I thought so, too," Skeeter said sadly. But he didn't say it until the kids had walked away.

Chapter Fifteen

For most people, the Sunny Vista Nottingham Hotel was a home away from home. For Skeeter, it was just plain home.

Until now.

He had twenty-four hours to clear out of his room. Which wasn't much time to pack up his whole life. By morning, he was only half done. There was a knock at the door. It was Wendy.

"Welcome back," Skeeter said, trying not to sound too miserable. "You mad at me?"

"Not as mad as Jill," Wendy said. "But mad. Yes."

"But I didn't know where the new hotel was going," Skeeter defended himself.

"I figured that," Wendy said tersely.

Skeeter didn't understand. "Then what? Because of all the junk food I gave the kids?"

"No. I figured you'd do that, too." Wendy's expression softened. She crossed the room and sat down on the edge of a twin bed. It was the one that used to belong to her, back when she was a little kid. "I'm mad because you told my kids, 'In real life there are no happy endings.'"

Skeeter laughed bitterly and pointed to the stack of moving boxes. "Look around, Wendy— do you see a happy ending here?"

Wendy did take a look around. But it wasn't the room she was seeing—it was the past. "You and Dad always had so much fun in this room," she told him. "For whatever reason, I didn't. I was the cynic, the sourpuss, the . . . uh . . ."

"The downer?" Skeeter suggested. "The black cloud, the energy drainer, the mood killer?"

Wendy hung her head. "Yes. All those things," she admitted. "But when I left Bobbi and Patrick with you, I secretly hoped that you would rub off on them. Get them to be light, to have fun, to enjoy things . . . to be more like you and Dad."

He glanced over at the picture frame sitting on top of one of the moving boxes. Skeeter would give anything to be able to ask his dad for some advice right now. But he was on his own.

"Well, anyway, I got a job in Arizona," Wendy continued. "Teaching, not principaling. You should come visit us when we get settled. I'm sure by then the kids would love to see you."

Skeeter tried to be happy for his sister and her kids. But he couldn't help feeling a pang of sadness that they would be moving so far away.

Wendy turned to leave but paused in the doorway. "By the way," she told Skeeter. "I had a chili dog in Phoenix—thought I'd died and gone to heaven."

Once his sister had left, Skeeter slumped into a chair and stared at the ceiling. He knew he should get back to packing, but he couldn't make himself do it. There was something way too depressing about taping up all those boxes. It was too final, like this was really it, the end of his story.

Wait a minute—Skeeter sat bolt upright.

His story.

This was *his* life, *his* story—which meant *he* should be the one to decide how it was going to end, right?

Skeeter asked himself what he would do if he were a character in one of the bedtime stories. If he were a *hero*.

Skeeter the hero would save the school. He would prove himself to his niece and nephew. And, Skeeter decided, he would most *definitely* plant a juicy kiss on the fairest maiden in the land.

Basically, Skeeter, the bedtime-stories hero would make himself a happy ending. And Skeeter, the real-world hero, was determined to do the same thing.

He just had to figure out how.

Chapter Sixteen

Kendall Duncan stood in front of the empty school wearing a shiny new hard hat. It was a big day for him: demolition day.

"Mr. Nottingham said he'd call if there was a problem getting the variance," he told his crew. "So if we don't hear from him in the next few minutes, we can go ahead and blow this dump up."

But over at City Hall, Mr. Nottingham *was*

having a problem. A big problem. And its name was Jill.

"Mr. Nottingham, I was wondering if I could speak to you for a minute," she said, as he climbed the steps toward city hall. "My name is Jill Hastings, and I'm a teacher at Webster Elementary."

He ignored her and walked faster.

"I'd just like to talk to you, as a person, for a minute." Jill struggled to stay polite as she ran to follow Barry into the elevator. "There must be many other possible sites for your hotel complex that would not result in the displacement of 350 hardworking students."

Mr. Nottingham continued to ignore her. Only when they came to the door marked DONNA HYNDE, COMMISSIONER OF ZONING did he finally face her. "Look, the war is over. You lost. I'm sorry." He didn't sound sorry as he stormed through the lobby of the zoning commissioner's office.

"This isn't a war, Mr. Nottingham. This is about the children," she called after him.

The zoning commissioner's secretary tried to explain that Ms. Hynde was busy with someone else, but Mr. Nottingham barreled into the commissioner's office anyway. When he arrived he found her deep in conversation—with Skeeter.

"What is *he* doing here?" Mr. Nottingham asked.

Jill's eyes widened. She hadn't realized that Commissioner Hynde was Skeeter's old high-school tormentor, the one Jill had met in the beachside tavern.

"Barry, Jill, we're just wrapping up," Skeeter said, leaning back in his chair and taking a sip of coffee. "Donna, you remember Jill, don't you?"

"Of course," Donna said, smiling at Jill. "I love those earrings."

"Thanks," Jill said. She was totally flummoxed.

"Bronson, what are you *doing* here?" Mr. Nottingham asked irritably.

"Yeah, what *are* you doing here?" Jill echoed.

Skeeter grinned, and winked at the commissioner. " Donna, tell these guys what I'm doing here."

Donna winked back. "Mr. Bronson is here

129

because, as a concerned citizen, he wanted to bring up several interesting points before I made any hasty decisions."

"It's true," Skeeter said, nodding. "I brought up several interesting points."

"Points that will probably take me several years to analyze," Donna added.

Mr. Nottingham's eyes bulged. *"Years?"* he repeated, his hands clenching into fists. "Are you playing hardball with me, Bronson?"

"Oh, I ain't playing," Skeeter responded triumphantly. "Your application for a variance has been . . ." he pointed at the commissioner.

"Denied," Donna said on cue.

"Denied," Skeeter confirmed. "But don't worry: me and Donna have found a great property for auction on the beach in Santa Monica that is uptight and outta-sight."

Mr. Nottingham was stunned. "Really? Beachside?"

Skeeter nodded and extended a hand. "Friends?"

"Germs," Mr. Nottingham reminded him, as he shrank away.

"Let's get past that," Skeeter said and hugged the hotel owner before he could object.

After a surprisingly drawn-out moment, Mr. Nottingham pulled away from the hug and took out his cell phone to call Kendall. It was time to stop the demolition once and for all.

"Did you really just fix everything?" Jill asked Skeeter as Mr. Nottingham dialed.

"Not everything," Skeeter said. "Not yet." But he was about to change that. He leaned toward Jill, brushed a strand of hair away from her face, and—

"Uh, we have a little bit of a situation," Mr. Nottingham interrupted. "I can't reach Kendall on his cell to halt the demolition."

"Well, can you call someone else who's there?" Skeeter asked.

Mr. Nottingham shook his head. "I did, and I'll keep trying. But so far, no luck." He dialed again—and again. But what he didn't realize was that

Kendall's engineers had set out radio-controlled explosives, a type of device that is very sensitive to cell phones. Everyone on-site had turned off their phones. There was no way to reach them—and no way to stop the demolition!

And what they also didn't realize was that at that exact moment, Patrick and Bobbi were sneaking through the abandoned school, carrying a giant homemade banner: THIS SKOOL IS AWESOME!

"When the demolition guys see this sign in the window, they'll change their minds," Bobbi said hopefully. Neither of them realized that with the touch of a button, Kendall could bring the whole building crashing down on their heads. Only Skeeter and Jill could save them.

If they could get there in time . . .

Chapter Seventeen

Skeeter and Jill rushed out of city hall. Jill led the way to her car, and they got to it just in time— just in time to see it being towed.

But there wasn't time to get upset about parking in a tow-away zone now.

"Where's your truck?" Jill asked.

"It ain't mine. The hotel took it back," Skeeter said with a shrug.

This was a disaster. It was hard enough getting

around L.A. *with* a car. Without one, there was no way. But Skeeter spotted something in the park across the street that he thought could help. "Come on!" he yelled.

Once they reached the park, they ducked behind a grove of bushes, just in time to watch two tough-looking bikers dismount their motorcycles in front of a hot-dog stand.

As the bikers paid for their hot dogs, Skeeter crept out from behind the bushes and climbed onto one of the motorcycles. Jill climbed on behind him, and the motorcycle roared to life. The bikers whirled around, but Skeeter and Jill were already gone.

Skeeter pressed the accelerator down as far as it would go. As they zoomed through the streets, Skeeter felt like *he* was Sir Fixalot astride his noble steed, Jillian the Mermaid's arms tight around his waist. He imagined them as Jeremiah and Miss Davenport, fighting off bandits and outrunning a wild mustang stampede. They were on a mission. Just like Skeetacus, the ancient warrior, and Skeeto, the galactic hero, he was destined to save the day. He was—

Stuck.

They screeched to a stop in front of a dusty set of train tracks. As the gate descended and the lights flashed, a long freight train thundered past. It seemed to stretch on forever—boxcar after boxcar, with no end in sight. Skeeter gunned the accelerator. They didn't have enough time to wait for the train to pass.

"What are you doing?" Jill cried, hanging on as tightly as she could.

Instead of answering, Skeeter headed for a nearby billboard, then expertly fishtailed into the bottom of it, breaking the base. It toppled over onto a car, forming a perfect ramp. He lined up the bike and revved the engine.

"Skeeter!" Jill shrieked in terror.

But Skeeter knew this was their only shot. He gripped the handlebars and accelerated. They hit the ramp and flew into the air—across the tracks and *through* a boxcar that had both of its doors open—then landed safely on the other side.

Now nothing could stop them. They barreled down the street toward the school. Soon the building came into sight.

A few protesters were milling about, and in the center of everything stood Kendall, looking triumphant.

"Twenty seconds!" Kendall yelled to the demolition team.

Wendy stood with some of the other school faculty. Suddenly, she realized Bobbi and Patrick were no longer at her side. Frantically, she started looking around the school yard for them.

"Wait," she called to Kendall. "I can't find my children! They might be in there!"

"Nice try," Kendall said with a disdainful sneer. "We cleared the building hours ago." He glanced at his watch. "Ten seconds!"

Skeeter pushed the motorcycle to its breaking point. He and Jill blew into the playground, where the demolition guys had set up all of their equipment. Jill grabbed hold of the monkey bars as they sped past, and she flew off the bike. Without her added weight, Skeeter was able to push the bike to go even faster.

Skeeter let go of the handlebars just as the bike passed the school-yard tetherball pole. He grabbed the tetherball, letting the bike speed on without him, and he spun around the pole toward Kendall.

Kendall's finger hovered over the switch.

Three . . . two . . . one . . .

Bull's-eye! Skeeter slammed into Kendall feet first, knocking him out of the way before he could set off the explosives. Kendall toppled backward just as Bobbi and Patrick burst out of the school building.

"What happened?" Bobbi asked, looking around at the excited crowd.

Skeeter swept his niece and nephew into a firm bear hug. "What happened is they decided not to blow up the school."

Patrick looked almost disappointed. "But we didn't even get to hang our sign!"

"They heard about it and that was enough to make them stop," Skeeter assured him. "You guys are heroes."

Patrick and Bobbi jumped up and down. As they were celebrating, a very pretty little girl around Patrick's age came running over. "How can I thank you for saving the school?" she asked Patrick.

Patrick grinned. "No thanks necessary . . . ma'am."

"There must be some way for me to show my appreciation," the little girl said. Then she leaned in and gave him a quick kiss on the cheek. Patrick's face turned a bright pink.

Skeeter turned to Bobbi, who was laughing at her brother's freak-out. "If someone's kissing Master Stinky, I should get a little mermaid action, right?" he asked Bobbi. She gave him the thumbs-up.

He looked at Jill, who smiled. That was all the encouragement he needed.

It was a fairy-tale kiss. A happily-ever-after kind of kiss. Except it was even better than any kiss in a story. Because this kiss was real.

Chapter Eighteen

Months later, Skeeter, Jill, Bobbi, and Patrick had another rooftop campout. The view from the roof of Marty's Motor Inn wasn't quite as grand as the one from the Sunny Vista Nottingham Hotel. But it was still beautiful. And, like the motel itself, it was special—because it belonged to Skeeter.

"I'm glad your mom let you spend the night tonight," Skeeter said, carefully roasting his marshmallow over the fire. "I know you guys missed me as much as I missed you."

"We missed Aunt Mermaid," Patrick said.

"And the s'mores," Bobbi pointed out.

Jill laughed. "Speaking of s'mores, I think Bugsy needs another one." The pet hamster was licking marshmallow goo off Jill's hands. "But we're out of marshmallows."

"That's not a problem," Skeeter said. "Room service!" he bellowed.

A few seconds later, Kendall appeared on the roof, looking neat and tidy in his room-service uniform. "Yes, sir?" he asked wearily.

"Can you get my friend Bugsy some more marshmallows?" Skeeter asked.

Kendall sighed. "Right away, sir. Is there anything else you need?"

"Not from you." He thought for a moment. "But . . . *housekeeping*!"

Aspen, the snotty (former) receptionist, came running around the corner. She was wearing a maid's uniform. "Yes, Mr. Bronson?"

"Please make sure that Bugsy's cage is cleaned before he checks out tomorrow," Skeeter said, suppressing a smile.

"Absolutely, Mr. Bronson," Aspen said bitterly.

"Thanks," Skeeter said. "And you know I like to be called Skeeter."

"Of course," Aspen said through gritted teeth, "*Skeeter.*"

Aspen and Kendall walked away together, equally miserable. Once they were gone, Skeeter relaxed again, leaning back and gazing up at the stars.

"Oooh, check that one!" Jill exclaimed. "It looks like a goat!"

"Wow, you know something? You are out of your mind," Skeeter teased. "That looks nothing like a goat."

Jill punched him playfully on the arm. Skeeter and the kids started laughing, and soon Jill joined in. Skeeter still couldn't believe that things had worked out so well. He was now the owner and operator of Marty's Motor Inn, thanks to a generous loan from Barry Nottingham, his former boss and current friend. Wendy had been able to keep her job at Webster Elementary, although the life-changing chili dog she ate in Arizona led to a much more relaxed attitude.

Bobbi and Patrick were thriving, as children often do when they are happy and well-loved.

And Skeeter and Jill? Well, it may sound like a fairy-tale cliché, but every once in a while, fairy-tale clichés come true. And Skeeter and Jill were living out the most famous cliché of all. The one where a goofy hotel handyman and a mermaid teacher fall in love and . . .

. . . live happily ever after.